The Flight of the Whisper King

BRADLEY BEAULIEU

First Edition: May 2020

ISBN: 978-1-93964-937-9 (Paperback)
ISBN: 978-1-93964-935-5 (epub)
ISBN: 978-1-93964-936-2 (Kindle)

Please visit me on the web at
http://www.quillings.com

Praise for *Twelve Kings in Sharakhai*

"As graceful and contemplative as it is action-packed and pulse-pound-ing.

—NPR Books

"Wise readers will hop on this train now, as the journey promises to be breathtaking."

—Robin Hobb, author of *The Assassin's Apprentice*

"This is an impressive performance."

—Publishers Weekly

"I am impressed... An exceedingly inventive story in a lushly realized dark setting that is not your uncle's Medieval Europe. I'll be looking forward to the next installment."

—Glen Cook, author of *The Black Company*

"Bradley P. Beaulieu's new fantasy epic is filled with memorable characters, enticing mysteries, and a world so rich in sensory detail that you can feel the desert breeze in your hair as you read. Çeda is hands-down one of the best heroines in the genre— strong, resourceful, and fiercely loyal to friends and family. Fantasy doesn't get better than this!"

—C. S. Friedman, author of the Magister trilogy

"Exotic, sumptuous and incredibly entertaining, Beaulieu has created memorable characters in a richly imagined world."

—Michael J. Sullivan, author of The Riyria Chronicles

"Beaulieu's intricate world-building and complex characters are quickly becoming the hallmarks of his writing, and if this opening volume is any indication, The Song of the Shattered Sands promises to be one of the next great fantasy epics."

—Jim Kellen, Science Fiction and Fantasy Book Buyer for Barnes & Noble

"Beaulieu's fantasy worlds are well-imagined and richly drawn...the kind you want to keep visiting."

—Kirkus Speculative Reading List

The Flight of the Whisper King

Mala stared with disbelief into the eyes of Arük, the magnetic but not-so-bright leader of their small gang, or flock, as they were often referred to in Sharakhai. "Forgive me, but I thought you just said you wanted to go to the garrison."

Arük, leaning against a mudbrick wall, grinned that broad grin of his. With his big ears and uncombed hair, he looked like a hyena trying to make friends. "I did, kitten. I did indeed." Arük knew very well she hated the nickname he'd given her, which was of course precisely why he used it.

"The garrison where all the Silver Spears live?" Mala asked. "*That* garrison?"

Arük laughed his deriding laugh, the one that made

1

him sound like a braying mule. As he pulled out his ram's head jambiya, the expensive knife with the curving blade he just *loved* to show off, he said, "Haven't you heard? The Malasani sent their golems storming through it. The Spears are all dead or gone, retreated to the House of Kings."

The two of them stood just outside the spice market along a stretch of road famed for its food carts. The street, just like the spice market and the bazaar and the streets all across the west end, was eerily vacant. Mala had never seen the like, but then again, it wasn't every day a foreign enemy fell upon the city like locusts.

The day's heat had been intense, a heat made all the worse by the sounds of battle that had consumed the city for hours. No one thought the walls of the city could be breached so easily, but the Malasani army had brought with them hundreds of golems. They'd stormed past the walls and pushed deep into the city before suddenly retreating to the city's sandy southern harbor near nightfall. With the bulk of the Silver Spears having already fled to the House of Kings and its high walls, and the city's populace waiting out the violence in their homes, the streets had been all but abandoned.

"The Spears may have left the garrison," Mala went on, "but they'll come back sooner or later."

Gripping his jambiya by the blade, a thing any fool

would know you're not supposed to do, Arük used the point to clean his fingernails. "I'm sure they will."

"They might be there right now."

"But they aren't." Arük grinned and jutted his chin toward the nearby archway, where his lanky second-in-command, Kasha, was swaggering toward them in that long-legged way of hers. More of their flock, three gutter wrens a few years older than Mala's eleven summers, trailed after her. "Kasha's been watching it since the golems stormed through. Haven't you, Kasha?"

Stone-faced as ever, Kasha nodded, as if she couldn't care less what Arük or Mala or anyone else thought. She stopped a few paces away. The three gutter wrens came to a stop as well and watched Arük expectantly.

With a nod like he'd just surveyed his kingdom and found nothing wanting, Arük pushed himself off the crumbling, mudbrick wall. "Let's go. I want to be in and out before the final hour."

His idea was simple: break into the garrison, plunder it for anything they could sell or trade, and get out. But Mala's worries were already growing. The garrison was the seat of power for the Silver Spears, the infantry who made up Sharakhai's city guard, the very soldiers who were fighting for the city's survival against its invaders, the Malasani horde and their army of clay golems.

It was a terrible, mud-brained idea, but what was

Mala to do? She was not only the youngest member of their flock, she was also the newest, a thing Arük constantly reminded her of—nothing she did or said was going to change his mind. So she walked in silence, wary of the crunching of their sandals against the dry ground. She listened for the rumble of approaching cavalry or foot soldiers, peered along every vacant avenue and through every stone archway for signs they were being watched.

When they reached the hulking stronghold, Mala's gut began to churn worse than it already was. The garrison was crude compared to the buildings around it, so much so that it looked incongruous, a glowering bull in a herd of graceful oryx. The front gates were intact, but when they headed around to the back they saw that the sturdy, reinforced service doors had been sundered, crashed inward, surely by blows from the massive golems. It was terrible luck. Mala had been hoping the garrison would be locked up tight.

As their small flock huddled some twenty paces from the entrance, Arük nodded to Mala. "Go on, then."

As she'd known he would, Arük was asking her to go in first. It was why she was part of their flock. Oh, she was decent enough with a blade, but she excelled at being quiet, at being *unseen*. There was something about this place, though. The garrison's darkened entrance looked like the maw of some mythical beast ready to devour her the moment she came near.

Arük shoved her into motion. "I said go *on*."

Mala glowered at him, then went through the silent ritual she always performed when a bit of sneaking was required. She drew the shadows around her, wove them tight, then wore the resulting darkness like a cloak. Her instincts screamed for her to run as she crept carefully toward the yawning black entryway. Like a fool, she quashed them and stepped inside.

Despite all Mala's worrying, Kasha was right. The garrison *was* empty—of the living, in any case. Men and women in the uniforms of the Silver Spears lay strewn about the stone floor, their white tabards filthy with dirt, blood, and gore. All were dead. The stink of it made Mala gag.

Dozens of corpses were concentrated around a large clay body, a golem from the war. Its *flesh*, which felt like potter's clay, dry but not *too* dry, was cut in dozens of places. A spear jutted from its chest. Mala stared at the carnage and shook her head. So many trained soldiers, and they'd only managed to kill a single golem.

The large room before her, lit in ghastly relief by the light filtering in through the broken door and several high windows, was clearly the armory. Weapons of all sorts—swords, spears, bows, arrows, war hammers, and more—hung on racks mounted to the walls. A smithy's table, complete with anvil, forge, and all manner of hammers and chisels, sat in one corner. She left the armory and searched the other rooms on the first and second floors. Finding them empty, she let go the shadows and waved Arük and the others in. They entered and began rooting among the dead, collecting necklaces and rings, digging through the leather purses strung to their belts. The dead soldiers had surprisingly little. A few silver six pieces, a handful of copper khet.

"A rahl!" said Rennek, holding the golden coin high for all to see. In the dim light, the golden coin was a near match for his tawny hair.

It was rather thick of him, Mala mused. If *she'd* found a rahl, she would have slipped it, with no one the wiser, beneath her trousers into the tiny pouch she'd sewn into her knickers. But she had surprisingly poor luck. She found a pile of coins, a silver necklace, a twisted copper torque, and a few rings, one with Bakhi's symbol stamped onto it, a ward against death—nothing worth risking a beating over.

She wondered about these men and women, the sort of lives they'd led. She wondered about those who'd survived them. They must have had wives or husbands they'd left behind, daughters and sons, lovers and friends. Gods, some of those were no doubt still unaware of the soldiers' deaths—their bodies had hardly cooled since the battle hours earlier, after all.

Then she came across the body of a girl who looked to be the same age as Jein, Mala's five-year-old sister. The girl wore a simple blue dress that was clean and well made and which, unlike the vast majority of the dirty, blood-stained clothes adorning the dead, was surprisingly pristine. The girl had no wound Mala could see, until she crept to her opposite side and saw that her skull was misshapen near the back, pressed inward, a blow from a golem's fist, perhaps.

Mala felt tears welling as she stared into the girl's lifeless brown eyes. Why had she come to the garrison? Had she been visiting her father? And how had she been caught inside the armory? Was the golem's attack so quick she'd had no chance to hide?

"Her, too."

Arük crouched several paces away, tugging hard on a man's ruby ring, which was apparently refusing to come off. He widened his eyes, pulled his jambiya, and used the tip to point at the dead girl. Seeing the tears in Mala's eyes, he shook his head and lowered his knife toward the dead man's ring finger.

Mala turned her back to him and made a show of checking the girl's corpse. She refused to so much as touch the girl's skin, however, or the cloth of her pretty dress. The girl might have passed on to the farther fields; that didn't mean Mala had the right to defile the body of one so young.

When they were done looting the armory, they lit lanterns and split up to search the other rooms. The garrison was poor in things like silver and gold, but there was plenty of value, medicines chief among them, but also papyrus, spices and cutlery from the kitchens, a lustrous aban board with pieces crafted from ivory, ebony, and red jasper.

"Down here!" came Kasha's voice from the floor below.

They all rushed down to the small room Kasha had found. Built into the wall directly across from the entryway was an impressively large metal door, a vault with a keyhole, mounted on hinges as big as Arük's balled up fists.

Kasha, wonder breaking across her normally rigid face, waved to it. "I reckon there's enough in there to let us live like Kings and Queens for the rest of our lives."

"Sure," said Arük, "but how do we get in?" He was gripping his knife, twisting it this way and that while glaring at the door as if it were as simple as prying the massive thing off its hinges. He must know that none of them were going to be able to open it. He must. Even Mala could see it was hopeless. How many thieves in the city could manage it? Three, maybe four? People an idiot street thief like Arük would never even have met.

"Did you see any crowbars in the armory?" Arük asked.

The others mumbled replies, some offering ideas of their own. Mala, meanwhile, rolled her eyes and stole away with a lantern, preferring to explore the rest of the lower floor. She checked several rooms before arriving at one filled with shelves upon shelves of books, a library of sorts or, given the similarity between many of the leatherbound books, the garrison's archives, the place where the Spears kept their annals.

"They're not *all* annals, though," Mala breathed. "There are other books here, too. Books filled with stories."

Mala's mother had taught her how to read when she was young, just like she was teaching Jein. They owned few enough books, but the ones they *did* have Mala had read dozens times. And here were hundreds more to choose from. Which to take, though? And how many would Arük *allow* her to take? He couldn't read and was jealous of those who could. He'd pestered Mala mercilessly for weeks after she'd brought a book with her on a day they were meant to run scams on the patrons in the bazaar.

He'd snatched it from her hands when he'd caught

her reading it, then threw it onto the dry, packed earth. "Leave it," he said. When she'd tried to pick it up, he'd shoved her back. "I said *leave it.*"

"But it's *mine.*"

"You can have it back when we're done."

"But that'll be *hours.* It'll be gone by then."

Arük had shaken his head. "I won't have it distracting you when we're here to earn money."

When she'd tried to pick it up anyway, he'd grabbed her and slapped her across the face. "It stays," he said, putting his hand on that ridiculous knife of his.

He proceeded to lead them to another area of the bazaar to purposely move away from the book. Mala had hoped no one would notice it, but of course they had. When she returned at the end of the day, it was gone.

In the depths of the garrison, she stared up at the shelves, stared at the bindings. She took a few down and paged through them, then chose two that looked to tell tales from myth, her favorite type of story. She'd just spotted a thick tome with a green snakeskin cover, and was wondering what sort of gems she might find in it— not to mention how she might manage to get it out without Arük's seeing it—when she sensed something wrong. Something odd.

Just as Mala was gifted with drawing shadows around her, she knew when she was being watched. She turned and shivered, let out a small squeak, for there, lying in the corner, was a woman in a battle dress and turban, both dyed rusty red. The dress itself was cut in the style of the Kings' Blade Maidens, but the Maidens all wore black.

So why is this one wearing red?

A name came to Mala: Kestrels, the fabled band of swordswomen who were more highly trained than even the legendary Blade Maidens. *She must be one of them,* Mala thought.

Mala approached the woman, thinking surely she must be dead. She had a host of small wounds on her arms and chest that appeared to have been hastily bound with bandages, all of which were stained the deep crimson of dried blood. Worse were the two arrows sticking out of her. One was wedged in her chest, the other in her left calf. The arrow shafts had been snapped off near the point of entry—an attempt to allow her free movement, perhaps?

When Mala came within two paces and lifted the lantern high, she realized the woman's chest was rising and falling with breath, though only shallowly. Oddly, there were a number of books lying on the floor. They'd clearly been toppled from the nearby shelves, though why that might be, and what the Kestrel might have been looking for, Mala had no idea.

11

When Mala swung her gaze back to the Kestrel, a terrible shiver ran down her frame. The woman's eyes were open. And the expression on her face... Gods, she looked like she wanted to draw her sword and cut Mala down. It made Mala stand up from her crouch and take a half-step back.

"Mala?"

It was Arük, calling from the other room. Mala was too frightened to utter a word, though.

"Mala?" Arük called, louder this time.

Without taking her eyes from the Kestrel, Mala swallowed and called, "Yeah?"

"Get back here. I need you to get some things from the armory."

"All right," she said, but remained rooted to the spot.

She should tell the others. She should tell them there was someone here, someone still alive. But if she did that, Arük would kill her. He'd say they couldn't afford to have any witnesses, and then he'd draw his jambiya and use it to slice the woman's throat. She thought about simply leaving, but the result would be the same: one of the others would come to this room eventually, either before or after their failed attempt at opening the vault, and kill her then.

She thought about dragging the Kestrel away, hiding her in a large foot locker or a wardrobe, but she didn't know if she could actually find a place that would remain untouched until they left. And besides, she wasn't sure if she could drag her anyway. The Kestrel was a woman fully grown. Mala was only eleven. And even if she *did* manage to hide her, the Kestrel's wounds would likely kill her. She needed a physic badly.

"Mala?" Arük's voice was louder, angrier. He was searching for her.

Staring into the woman's eyes, Mala shrugged, shook her head. She didn't know what to do.

The Kestrel stared beyond Mala at the open door, then gazed up at the shelves, above the gap where the books on the floor had once been. She licked her lips, swallowed, then seemed to come to some sort of decision. She lifted one arm and pointed to the highest shelf. "The blue one," she whispered, "pull it."

Mala had no idea what she meant—what earthly good would pulling a book from the shelf do?—but she could hear Arük's footsteps coming closer. She had only seconds in which to act. Deciding the Kestrel must know what she was doing, Mala pulled the blue book and heard a click, and the shelf swung outward ever so slightly. A hidden passage, Mala realized, a thing she thought only existed in books. She pulled the shelf out to reveal a dark passageway.

The Kestrel held out one arm. "Help me in."

Arük's footsteps were close. They were heavy. Clomping. Angry.

Mala took the woman's arm and pulled with all her might, but the going was too slow. Arük was going to arrive at any moment. He would enter the room and see the Kestrel. And then he'd kill her and likely beat Mala for the trouble.

She pulled harder and managed to get her halfway into the passage, then all the way. As she stepped out and pushed the shelf closed, she caught a glimpse of the Kestrel's face—worry mixed with gratitude. Then she clicked the shelf shut just as Arük came strutting in.

"What sort of mud has gotten into that skull of yours, Mala? I said I needed you." He stared at the books—the ones on the shelves and the ones on the floor. "Oh, not *that* again."

Mala breathed a sigh of relief. He thought she'd been caught up in the books. To complete the ruse, she took up the ones she'd found earlier, knowing precisely what was going to happen next.

True to form, Arük slapped them from her hands, then slapped *her* upside the head. "Go to the smithy's table we saw upstairs. Grab any crowbars you find, plus hammers and chisels."

Her ear stinging from the slap, Mala picked up her lantern and left, but not before sending a quick glance toward the far corner of the room. The Kestrel would likely die, but at least she wouldn't die because *Mala* hadn't tried to save her.

Bright, burning pain woke Shohreh from unconsciousness, which was ironic since it was the pain that had caused her to pass out in the first place. She lay in darkness just inside the hidden passageway beneath the garrison. The girl, some street thief from the looks of her, had dragged her from where she'd fallen unconscious in the annalist's room, deposited her in the passageway, and left. And not a moment too soon. The girl had been speaking with someone. Shohreh hadn't been able to hear the words—she'd deafened herself on the orders of King Zeheb, the Whisper King, years ago— but the look on the girl's face had told Shohreh all she needed to know. The girl had been worried that she'd be discovered sheltering a Kestrel, which meant that the one calling for her would likely have killed Shohreh where she lay and punished the girl for her deceit after.

It made a strange sort of sense that it was a handful of gutter wrens who'd decided to descend on the garrison like locusts. Any of the larger gangs that ran the city's west end would think twice about stealing from the

Silver Spears—they knew the sort of reprisals that would come were it discovered that they'd set a single foot inside the garrison's walls. A flock of young ones, though, unattached to a larger gang? They just might be dumb enough to do it.

They'd get their due. The Crone would make sure of it. The Crone was, after all, akin to a hidden monarch, a buried queen, and the garrison was for all intents and purposes the upper reaches of her palace. She was the House of Maidens' High Matron, the ancient woman Shohreh had been trying to reach when she'd fallen unconscious, and she would brook no insult like this, not without a measure of blood to balance the scales.

With a grunt Shohreh failed to stifle completely, she levered herself up against the cold stone wall. Stars filled her vision, but she managed to keep her feet, thank the gods. Each limping step she took along the passageway made the pain in her calf flare. She tried hopping on the other leg to lessen the pain, but that only fanned the flames of pain from the arrow buried in her chest. The stars came rushing back. Her vision swam until she stopped, took slow breaths, and waited for the spell to pass. It was a near thing, and more grave than she wanted to admit. Pass out again and surely the lord of all things would tire of the game and come for her.

With painstaking care, she wended her way along

winding passages that grew more mazelike the closer she came to the Crone's lair. Eventually she saw a dim light, heard the crackle of a fire, smelled the strong incense the Crone preferred: river iris with a faint but distinct note of black lotus.

She came to a large room that had been carved from the stone in precise, square angles. Hanging around the room were all manner of maps. Some were old, some were new. Some were of Sharakhai, others of the kingdoms that bordered Great Shangazi. Many detailed the desert itself, or parts of it. All were lovingly framed, all lovingly cared for.

In the center of the room was the massive, round table that held a topographical rendering of Sharakhai. Every street, every building was rendered in sandstone, carved by the Crone herself after taking painstaking measurements on one of her forays into the city. Beneath the tabletop were seven drawers that could be pulled out to reveal the hidden byways beneath the city. Each drawer corresponded to a certain level of depth, and revealed all known structures: manmade tunnels, natural caverns, secret grottos. Even this place, the Crone's own inner sanctum, had been meticulously rendered there.

The way a city grows or shrinks, the Crone had once told Shohreh, *and how quickly it does so, tells you as much about its history as any text ever written.*

The map room was the place Shohreh most associated with her life after becoming an acolyte at the age of eight and, later, a fully fledged Kestrel. It was the place where the Kestrels received their missions, the Crone often using the maps to direct them. The room was empty, however, the Crone missing. Shohreh nearly laughed. She'd come all this way—from the slopes of Tauriyat, where King Ihsan had ordered his Silver Spears to slay her, to the walls around the House of Kings, to city streets thick with fighting, to the garrison itself, shortly after the pitched battle with the golems—only to find the one woman who could save her gone.

Had the Crone been called away by the Kings? Had she gone to learn news of the invasion? There was no telling, but it was inconvenient at best. Shohreh didn't want to die again. She'd done so three times already and each time was worse than the last. She didn't want to experience that pain again. She didn't want to go through the madness that accompanied her reawakening.

But what could she do? Staring into the fire in the hearth, she reckoned a bit of warmth would be nice after the grasping cold of the tunnels. *It's as good a place to die as any,* she thought as she limped toward it.

She made it only halfway before collapsing on the carpeted floor.

When Shohreh woke again, it was to a rocking sensation. She was being carried by someone with a heavy, lumbering gait. Who, though?

With great effort, she managed to lift her head to find the Crone herself carrying her like a baby.

The Crone had wrinkled skin and a severe expression on her dour face. A starburst tattoo marked the center of her broad brow. Another tattoo of a constellation—the one she'd been born under, Shohreh assumed—spiraled like a threatened cobra on her right cheek. A veritable bazaar's worth of jewelry adorned her ample frame. She had a silver headdress, a cascade of necklaces, a host of earrings, nose rings, and bracelets glinting under the light of the lamps being held by the cadre of young girls following in her wake.

The girls were the Crone's acolytes, her fledglings, those who might one day prove themselves skilled enough to become Kestrels like Shohreh. They watched with keen interest—*benign* interest, Shohreh was sure, though just then they looked like a pack of hungry jackals, each hoping Shohreh might fall that *she* might take her place.

Sülten, the eldest of them, held Shohreh's gaze. "*All will be well,*" she said. Shohreh couldn't hear her words, but she'd long since learned how to read lips. "*The Crone will save you.*"

In her bewilderment, Shohreh thought she was being carried to her own room to rest, to sleep for a time, but it soon became clear they were heading toward another room entirely. They passed beyond the rooms reserved for Shohreh and her sisters in arms, headed along a dark passage, and arrived at a large, circular room with a high ceiling: the Sepulchre.

The Sepulchre's ceiling was supported by nine spiraling stone columns. Between the columns, at the room's exact center, was a pit that looked like a grave waiting to be filled. Flanking the pit were a pair of large stone basins on stout iron legs, each filled to the top with ochre sand. A set of well worn shovels, brooms, and metal dust pans leaned against the basins.

This room was a special place in Sharakhai, a special place in the desert, and yet only a bare handful knew of its existence. It was where Shohreh had died as an acolyte and been reborn as a Kestrel. It was where she'd awoken two times since being slain, her body retrieved and returned there by her sister Kestrels.

When the Crone reached the side of the pit, she dropped to her knees with a grunt—a thing Shohreh was unable to hear but could easily feel resonating in her chest. After lowering Shohreh onto the stone floor, the

Crone motioned for the girls to disrobe her. The girls complied with efficient haste, tugging at the ties of Shohreh's battle dress and the laces of her tall leather boots.

The Crone, meanwhile, stared down at Shohreh stonily. *"Hold still, child. It will all be over soon."*

When Shohreh lay naked on the stone, the Crone flicked a hand to Sülten and accepted from her a wooden box. Within the box were a set of gleaming surgical instruments that she proceeded to apply to the flesh around the arrow shaft wedged deep in Shohreh's calf.

The pain that followed was deep and strong as the Haddah in spring. Shohreh grit her teeth against it. She shivered from head to toe. She refused to scream, however, refused to so much as moan. She concentrated instead on the curving wall, on the frieze near the ceiling that showed a gathering of old gods dancing a ring around Tauriyat as the sun crested the horizon.

With dogged efficiency, the Crone liberated the first arrowhead, then bent her attention to the second, the one in Shohreh's chest. Shohreh tried to bear the extraction in the same manner as she had the first, but the arrowhead, the sort of wicked device that was disinclined to be liberated from flesh once buried, caught against the ends of her broken ribs. This time Shohreh *did* scream. She felt weak for it, embarrassed before the

21

Crone and the young ones—she always tried to provide a good example, and here she was showing weakness against pain she knew very well how to combat.

Daring a glance, she found the fledglings watching her with varying amounts of horror, all save Sülten, who gazed down with much the same look as the Crone, eyes hard, lips curled in disdain.

Finally, blessedly, it was over, and Shohreh was left with an all-consuming ache and the feeling of warm blood trickling down her skin. Then the Crone lifted her and lowered her into the grave.

"Quickly now," she said to the girls.

"Yes, High Matron," the girls replied.

Their shovels at the ready, they used them to dig into the ochre sand in the stone basins situated on either side of the pit. Shovelfuls of sand thudded against her chest, her waist, her legs and her head. She felt its grit as it weighed her down and pressed her against the hard stone. Her blood mixed with the dry sand, adding a fresh dosing of red, which was the precise reason it was colored ochre—the sand had once been the natural amber color of the desert, or so the Crone had told her.

It was said that the sand was once a block of simple sandstone. Cut and liberated from the site of fallen Iri, one of the elder gods, after he'd left this world for the farther fields, the stone had been pulverized, and the resulting sand was found to return the dead to life. How long it would continue do so Shohreh had no idea, perhaps until the end of days.

Ever harder the sand pressed, robbing Shohreh of breath. It was a strangely comforting thing. She and death were no strangers, after all, and she found the idea of being released from her pain a sweet and heady thing.

So it was that as she let her breath go, she did so as she might with a dear friend: with a fond farewell, knowing their parting would be brief.

Shohreh woke with a sharp inhalation that tickled her throat even as it filled her lungs with sudden, sweet breath. The screaming in her mind faded, as did the wild dreams that always accompanied her rebirths. It felt like it went on for hours, though she was certain it was much less. As the dreams faded at last, a keen ringing filled her ears, a phantom sound, a strange visitation that harkened back to the days when she could still hear.

The fledglings were gone. Only the Crone remained. As had been true the other times she'd awoken in the Sepulchre, the grave was completely empty of sand. The fledglings had removed it. Shohreh herself had been painstakingly cleaned so that none of the precious sand was lost. It was back in the basins, awaiting the next Kestrel to die or, if her body couldn't be recovered, an acolyte ready to take her place.

As had been true in the past, Shohreh was still deaf. The sand, for whatever reason, never healed old wounds, only those received recently, which was one of the reasons, she supposed, the Kings had never used it. Well, that and the fact that each rebirth seemed to steal a bit of vitality from one's soul. What did the Kings need with such things, anyway? They were practically immortal, granted long life and vigor by the gods themselves.

As it should be, Shohreh thought. The Kings weren't perfect, no mortal was, but their rule had been anointed by the gods. They'd seen Sharakhai through four centuries of peril and threat. Gods willing, they'd see it through another four and more beyond.

The Crone held out a hand. *"Up."*

Shohreh gripped her hand, and the Crone helped her to her feet. Nearby was a wooden rack with a dress laid over it—not her red battle dress, but a sensible blue abaya. Shohreh donned it, then the leather sandals at the base of the rack. Finally, she tied her long, dark brown hair back and wrapped a white hijab around her head and shoulders. The clothes were welcome. The cold of the Sepulchre was rushing back now that she'd awoken fully. So was the familiar ache, the uncomfortable sensation that felt like her flesh was being stretched over a rack, ready to dry in the sun. The feeling would intensify soon. It would reach down into her muscles, her bones, discomfort blossoming into an ache that would debilitate her for days, a malady that grew worse each time she was reborn.

Holding Shohreh's hand in hers, the Crone led her to the map room, where a lively fire flickered in the hearth. After depositing Shohreh in one of the padded chairs near the fire, the Crone sat in the other, the one whose padding had long since molded itself to her shape. The fire's warmth was welcome, but a touch of sadness accompanied the feel of it on Shohreh's skin—she'd long since resigned herself to her loss of hearing, but gods how she missed the crackle of a fire.

She went on to tell the Crone of her mission, how Çedamihn and her Blade Maiden allies had been flushed from Eventide, the highest of the thirteen palaces on Tauriyat, how Shohreh had given chase, how King Ihsan had shown up, dressed as a captain of the Silver Spears of all things, and ordered his men to shoot her through with arrows.

The Crone listened with only half an ear, which felt like a betrayal—breath of the desert, a King had ordered a Kestrel to be murdered! When the story was done, she said to Shohreh, *"Ihsan's fate will have to wait. He was taken by the Malasani. It was thought he'd died in a smaller battle in the northern harbor, ridding us of one thorn in our side, but whispers have come. The golems took him and delivered him to the Malasani King himself."*

"Let me go, then, High Matron. I'll find him wherever they've stowed him and slit his throat as he sleeps."

"No," the Crone said flatly. *"We have more to worry about."*

"But—"

"I said no." Dour-faced, the Crone licked her teeth, her deeply wrinkled lips mounding as she did so. *"You have no idea how dire things have become. War has arrived in the streets of Sharakhai. None can say how the coming battles will play out, but with so many of the elder Kings dead, some are hoping to use it to raise their standing. And now this…"*

The Crone handed a stiff sheet of papyrus to Shohreh. On it were various entries written in clear, precise script. Each entry contained a few words, a sentence, sometimes a short paragraph. All had dates and times written next to them, indicating when each of the entries had been recorded. Shohreh was familiar with these sheets. They were transcriptions of King Zeheb's ravings. Zeheb had been driven mad by listening too closely to the whispers, conversations heard from afar that most thought to be secret.

There was once a time when all in Sharakhai feared being overheard by him. He'd been a powerful ruler, then, and a truly impressive man. The Crone and her Kestrels had all reported to him, often being sent on missions to verify the whispers he'd heard or to act on them. Shohreh had been proud to serve him and, through that service, help lift Sharakhai to greatness. She'd dedicated her life to it. She'd been *glad* to put out her ears so that Zeheb would have some measure of protection against Ihsan, the King with the honeyed tongue who Zeheb feared would one day move against him.

Much had changed since those days, when Zeheb's sun had shone its brightest. Many of the Kings lay dead; they'd been *given back to the desert*, as the saying went, several at the hands of Çedamihn the White Wolf. The Crone hardly knew which King she reported to anymore. When Zeheb had gone mad, the chain of command had been handed to King Husamettín and, after *he'd* been lost in the desert, to Kiral the King of Kings. Even Meryam, the Qaimiri Queen, told the Crone what to do from time to time, a privilege King Kiral allowed and the Crone despised.

Zeheb, meanwhile, had been reduced to this: tomes filled with random snippets of conversation or sometimes lone words whispered within his cell, all of them unattributed because Zeheb no longer had the presence of mind to say who had spoken them. It was why many had begun calling him foul names like the Burbling King or the Mad Bull of Sharakhai.

Shohreh read each of the entries, confused as to why the Crone had given it to her, until she came to the second to last. *On the night of moonless skies will they kill the Whispering King.* It sounded more like prophecy but wasn't. Zeheb did this sometimes, encapsulating conversations instead of repeating them verbatim.

Shohreh looked more closely at the dates. "These were recorded three days ago."

"Just so," said the Crone.

"You're taking this seriously?"

"We must."

"But the moonless night was last night. I assume he's still alive?"

"He is, but that may have been because word of this particular whisper had spread. The transcriber noticed and alerted both Zeheb's house and the other Kings. Precautions were taken." The Crone pointed to the sheet. *"Whoever planned on killing him last night would surely have delayed their plans once they learned of it."*

Shohreh flipped the papyrus over, hoping to find more clues about who he'd been listening to when he'd spoken those words. "It could be anyone," she finally said.

The Crone nodded. *"It may be, but I've since learned more. This morning, I spoke with our Lord King's daughter, Anann. The King's own house abounds with rumors that her*

28

brother, Temel, wishes to formally declare his standing as a King of the city. It is blasphemy, plain and simple. Our King, not yet taken to his final rest, lies trapped beneath Eventide. Temel has been satisfied to leave him there thus far, but no longer. Not with the chaos caused by the war and the fact that his father's crown remains unworn. Anann fears he is the one Zeheb was referring to, and that he will try to have Zeheb killed, and soon, so that his claim to the throne goes unquestioned."

For more than four centuries, King Zeheb had commanded the Crone and, through her, the Kestrels. He was also the Crone's father, and she was fiercely loyal to him. She prayed daily for his return to sanity. It made sense, then, that she would want to see him safely protected against such a threat. But—

"Temel was always loyal to his father," Shohreh said.

"True, but power blinds, my pretty little bird. Never forget that. A treasure he never thought to call his own now stands before him, and the only thing keeping him from it is his father's tenuous hold on life. We must protect Zeheb from this threat. You must protect him."

"I will do my best, of course"—she waved beyond the hearth, toward the Sepulchre—"but you know what it's like after waking." It was already growing worse, the feeling of tightness in her muscles, the ache. "Are any of my sisters near? Can I depend on their aid?"

The Crone shook her head, a motion that sent her host of silver earrings to swaying. The Kestrels of Sharakhai numbered nine in all, but most had been sent on missions to blunt the advance of Mirea or to gather intelligence on the Malasani army's weaknesses. *"They're all gone,"* said the Crone. *"I fear several are dead. You must do this alone, Shohreh. You will save our Lord King, by any means necessary. Make it your sole focus."*

Shohreh rolled her shoulders, trying and failing to work away the soreness. She was just about to ask for the particulars—what was known of Zeheb's situation in Eventide, where he was being kept, and the like—when she felt something at the edge of perception.

She turned and stared through the arched entryway, the very one she'd stepped through hours ago after making her way from the garrison. She was met with only darkness, but something felt strange. As was true of the Blade Maidens, Kestrels were taught how to feel for heartbeats. Shohreh did so now, reaching out, searching for the answer to this curious riddle. Even focusing so carefully, it took her long moments, but eventually she felt it, the faintest of heartbeats. It seemed distant, but Shohreh knew it wasn't so. Someone was masking themselves from her.

Whoever it was must have sensed her searching— why else would their heartbeat have spiked so? Then, of a sudden, she was there, her wide eyes and round face lit faintly by the ruddy glow of the fire. It was the girl. The one from the archives. Realizing she'd been unmasked, she sprinted away.

Part of Shohreh wished the Crone hadn't seen. Part of her wished that stupid, curious girl could go free and live out whatever life the fates had in store for her. But those were dreams of a more innocent world, dreams that were banished when the Crone turned her gaze away from the now-empty archway, fixed her furious stare on

Shohreh, and uttered two simple, devastating words.
"Kill her."

Mala sprinted along dark passageways, wending her way back the way she'd come, pulling the darkness around herself as tightly as she could.

Why had she gone back to the garrison? Why had she returned to the archives and like a mud-brained fool entered the tunnel where she'd left the Kestrel? Why had she continued until she'd heard the voices?

Stupid, Mala. Stupid, stupid, stupid.

She'd just been so curious over the woman's fate. She thought maybe she might get a reward after Arük robbed her of hers.

"You're new," Arük had said when they'd met a few hours later outside the bazaar to split the earnings from the garrison. "This is how it works, kitten. You start out, you pay your dues, you get paid when you've proven yourself. Isn't that right?" he asked Kasha.

Kasha, looking more than a little like a hook-nosed turtle under the faint light of the crescent moons, shrugged noncommittally, then gave a nod that spoke of unadulterated indifference.

Arük mugged a smile. "See?"

"She's just nodding because she knows it's what you want to hear. I went. I made sure it was safe before you came in. I collected money and gave it to you. I got your stupid crowbars and your stupid chisels, which we all knew was going to do fuck all against that vault door."

Arük dug in his purse and took out a handful of tarnished copper khet. "Here's something to tide you over."

The way he said it, like he was doing her a favor, made Mala so angry she slapped the coins out of his hand. "I deserve more. I *need* more."

Arük's face turned hard. "Remember your place, kitten. You're the youngest in this flock of ours. You've got potential, I'll grant you, with that little trick of yours. You get to be older, maybe take my place after I've moved on to bigger and better things, *then* you get the leopard's share of things. Until then…" He looked meaningfully at the coins glinting in the dirt. "Unless you want to go back to running the streets like a dirty little gutter wren."

He stood there, waiting for an answer. Mala wanted to punch him in the nose for it. She wanted to pull that ridiculous knife of his and cut him as he'd forced *her* to cut a woman just to enter the ranks of his flock. But she needed the paltry money that working for Arük brought in. She had a sister and a mother to take care of.

Breathing hard, she stooped and began picking up

the coins.

"Thought so," Arük said, and walked away. The others followed, several sending predatory smiles in Mala's direction before turning their backs on her.

Mala returned to her home in the Shallows to find her mother, Sirina, still awake. She was sitting in her rocking chair. Her dress was pulled up to her thighs and she was rubbing the dark spots on her swollen knees. The spots, swelling, and pain she'd been experiencing for weeks were signs of Bakhi's curse, a disease that had swept angrily through the Shallows, the largest neighborhood in the city's western quarter and the poorest by far.

Her mother swallowed hard. She looked at Mala expectantly. "So?"

Mala closed her eyes and opened her hand, revealing her paltry take. When she'd summoned the courage to open her eyes again, she knew what she would see, but the vision still gutted her. Her mother's eyes had gone red. Tears were forming.

They'd been trying to save up for a medallion from Bakhi's temple that would heal her affliction, a special medallion that came with a blessing from the priests. It was expensive, though. Day after day with the affliction growing worse, Memma had been unable to work at the carpetmaker's and Mala's take from her days running scams with Arük had brought in little more than what she'd once got begging with a cup along the edges of the bazaar. They were barely bringing in enough to feed themselves.

"Go see Ganesh in the morning," her mother said. "Use it for chickpeas and lemon and flour, a bag of rice if there's any left over."

It was a relief. Mala thought she'd been about to ask her to buy a bottle of araq so she could drown her pain in liquor. "Couldn't we go to the King's men now? Surely they'd give us *something*."

Mala's father had been a simple laborer in the city quarry—a laborer and one-time thief, her mother had admitted late one night during a drunken binge. "He said he used to wear shadows around him when he stole about," her mother said in one long slur, "which is absolute rubbish. If he could do that, why wasn't he the richest man in the city? Why did he never lavish me with pearls?"

After her mother had admitted his life as a thief to her, Mala had asked around the Shallows. He'd been caught trying to thieve from a drug lord. His left hand had been lopped off as punishment, and he'd been told were he to be caught again, not only would *he* die, but one of his daughters would as well. "The drug lord even told him he'd get to decide which one before he killed him!" the old storyteller had told Mala, as if it hadn't even occurred to him how terrifying it might be for the girl standing before him.

Before hearing that story, Mala had often considered telling her mother about her ability to weave shadows, a power she'd apparently inherited from her father, but after hearing what had happened to him, she swore she'd never tell anyone, not even Jein. Arük knew, but only because she'd used it so often in service to the flock.

Her father was long since dead, the victim of a fall in the quarry, and had left no inheritance save a sizable tab at the nearby oud parlor that Mother had been forced to pay. *Jein's* father, however, was none other than King Mesut. She was an illegitimate child, a bastard, but even so...

"The House of Kings would give us nothing but misery and woe." Before Mala could object, she went on. "Chickpeas, lemon, and flour, and a bag of rice if there's any left over."

"Yes, Memma."

Her mother hardly paid attention to Mala's reply. She'd gone back to rubbing her knees and rocking back and forth with a pained expression on her face. Mala tried to sleep, but she shared a bed with her little sister, Jein, who woke when Mala slipped into bed.

"I missed you," Jein whispered sleepily while

snuggling closer.

"I missed you, too," Mala whispered back.

Jein fell back to sleep quickly, but she had restless legs and kept kicking Mala beneath the blankets. With that and her mother's moaning, Mala was a thousand leagues from the land of dreams.

Visions of the Kestrel haunted her. Mala wondered if she'd died. Maybe she hadn't. Maybe she needed help. Maybe if Mala gave her some, she might give Mala a reward. And even if she didn't, Mala might still scavenge the garrison for *something* to sell.

With that faint hope in mind, she'd returned to the garrison. With the coming dawn a warm promise along the eastern horizon, she'd snuck in and found it still blessedly empty. After pulling the darkness around her, tight as a funeral shroud, she wended her way down to the archives, opened the door in the bookshelf, and walked along the tunnel. She'd found rooms. People *lived* there, deep below the city. Transfixed by her own curiosity, she'd gone farther and eventually heard voices. She came to a room that looked like a mausoleum. It was circular and had stout columns, intricately carved friezes on the walls and, in the center of the room, what looked to be an open grave. Within the pit was the woman, the Kestrel, naked as the day the desert had breathed life into her.

Beside the pit, an old, heavyset woman with enough jewelry to weigh down a pack mule was speaking to the Kestrel. She helped the Kestrel to stand and, wonder of wonders, her wounds had been healed! Instead of arrow shafts sticking from her flesh, she had only two angry, puckered scars on her bronze skin.

Mala should have left then. She should have backed away and returned to the garrison. She courted ruin by remaining. But this was all so very strange. She wanted to learn what had happened. She wanted to know who the old woman was. She wanted to know what would become of the Kestrel. So she followed them. She listened to their conversation in the room with the maps, how King Zeheb was in danger, how they planned to steal him away from Eventide in order to save his life.

But the fates, ever cruel in their ways, conspired against her. It was the very realization that she would be killed were it discovered that the she knew the information being passed between the two women that caused Mala's concentration to slip. The moment it did, the Kestrel's head snapped to where Mala was crouched within the passageway.

Knowing she'd been spotted, Mala turned and ran, faster than she'd ever ran before. The Kestrels were stronger than bone crushers, could run faster than a sprinting akhala, so how Mala made it beyond those subterranean passages to reach the garrison proper, she couldn't say. She knew one thing, though: Bakhi had smiled on her that day. As she reached the crisp morning air and began sprinting along the streets of the old city, she promised herself she'd go to Bakhi's temple and offer up a bit of copper, even if he *had* cursed Memma.

She knew she couldn't go home—the chances of the Kestrel somehow following her trail was too high—so she went to Arük's home instead, the one he shared with his senile old grandfather. Kasha and Rennek were there too, the three of them lounging on massive horsehair pillows. Between them, on a small, round table, was the best of the loot they'd taken from the garrison. Given the three small piles near their feet, it was clear they were divvying up the spoils. They also had a bottle of cheap, piss-yellow araq at hand. Each of them had a glass of it to call their own. This was a celebration, she realized. Arük clearly thought this some grand occasion.

"Can we talk?" Mala asked him.

"Not if it's about your share, kitten."

"Stop calling me kitten. And it's not about that."

"What, then?"

Mala's gut had already been roiling, but now it was threatening to boil over. "I don't want to say."

Arük laughed his biting laugh. "You don't want to *say?*"

She waved to Rennek and Kasha. "Not in front of them."

At this, Arük picked up his glass of araq, downed the lot of it, and sent the glass to clacking on the table. "Anything you want to say to me you can say to them."

All three waited, staring, uncaring, while Mala fumbled with her words. "I'm in trouble," she finally said. "I need a place to hide."

"What are you saying?"

"I went back," Mala mumbled.

"What?"

"I went *back*."

Arük's heavy brows lowered. A storm was building inside him. "To the *garrison*?"

Mala nodded and told them about finding the Kestrel, about helping her into the passageway and returning to find the Kestrel reborn, about how she'd been spotted and the Crone had commanded the Kestrel to kill her.

Arük flung one hand in the air. "Enough! Not one more word, Mala!" The expression on his face was no longer one of anger, but of abject fear. He looked every bit as scared as Mala. "First you lie to protect a bloody *Kestrel*—that was enough to put us all in danger, you know that, don't you? But that wasn't good enough, oh, no! You had to go back, and instead of leaving when you should've, you let them *see* you. And now you have the gall to come here and tell *us* the story?"

"The old woman ordered her to come for *me*, not you."

"You think the Kestrel will stop at your death once she learns you've told others?"

"How would she know?"

"Gods willing she never will!" Arük stood and stalked toward her. He was a whirlwind of fury and righteous purpose. He grabbed her by the neck, marched her through the door, and threw her onto the narrow, dusty alley.

Mala turned over, feeling betrayed and utterly lost. "I need *protection*. That's what a flock is for!"

Arük loomed over her while Rennek and Kasha stared from the doorway. "You don't *get* protection, not when you've betrayed us."

"I need a place to hide," she called as he stalked away.

"Use your little trick!" he called over his shoulder, then walked back inside his grandfather's home and slammed the door, leaving Mala lying there on the dirt.

Hardly a moment had passed before Mala felt laid bare before those who'd witnessed the exchange. Women stared down from the ranks of windows above. Two men eyed her from a darkened archway. Had they heard? Would one of them sell her out to the Silver Spears?

She was terrified of being alone in the streets, but she knew she couldn't go home. Arük had been right. She *had* put them in danger by going to them. Go home and she'd put her mother and sister at risk too, more than they already were. She'd lie low in one of her old hiding places in the spice market; she'd return home at night and convince her mother they needed to stay with aunt Mindra for a time.

Ignoring the stares from the windows and the archways, she headed down one of the narrow, winding alleyways the Shallows was famed for. The moment she was alone, she pulled the shadows close. More than simply a way to avoid being seen, the shadows were a balm against her fears. The Kestrel would move on to other things when she was unable to find Mala. Mala was certain of it.

Her heart lifted ever so slightly, she headed for the end of the alley, but pulled up short when the path ahead was suddenly blocked by a woman wearing a white hijab and a blue abaya with elegant, winglike sleeves, the very clothes the Kestrel had donned after rising from the pit.

Mala was normally good at sensing danger. She'd always been the first to run when the Spears or local enforcers or rival flocks showed up, and once she started running, she rarely got caught. Standing there before the Kestrel, however, she felt useless, a lamb gone stiff under the stare of a black laugher.

The Kestrel, however, wasn't looking at Mala with anger in her eyes. Rather, she looked intensely curious, like a collector of rare birds who'd discovered some new, previously unknown breed of river finch. "How do you do it?" she asked.

"Do what?" Mala stammered.

She waved to the alley around them, to the shadows. "Hide like you do."

Mala paused, not wanting to give away her secret, but visions of what the Kestrel would do to her were she to remain silent soon eclipsed those fears. "I've always been able to do it."

The Kestrel seemed to be watching Mala's lips closely, like Sama'an the deaf beggar did whenever someone spoke to him. "I asked you *how*, not how long."

What could Mala say? "I pull the shadows close and people look away."

"Can you do it whenever you want?"

She was staring so intensely at Mala's lips it made her uncomfortable. "Can you hear?"

The woman frowned. "Just answer the question."

Mala swallowed, embarrassed. "Yes."

"Good, because you're going to do it for me."

"What?" Mala was dumbstruck. "Why? Where?"

"We'll not speak of that here."

42

"But the old woman. She ordered you to kill me. I heard her."

"I owe you a life, little one, and I've had quite enough of killing innocents for the time being. Now, come with me. One of your Kings needs you." With that she turned and walked away, expecting Mala to follow.

Mala's fears hadn't ebbed in the least. She was nearly as afraid of what the Kestrel wanted her to do as she was of the consequences of not doing it. She could run away. She could try to hide. But what good would that do? The Kestrel had already found her once.

Swallowing her fears, she trailed after the Kestrel.

Mala's power over shadow was far from absolute. It was all but useless in patches of bright light, or suffused light like often came during the desert's rainy season. The spell could be broken if she grew careless and moved too quickly or allowed her footfalls to make too much noise. She could be spotted if her clothes clashed with her surroundings, which was why she often wore muddy colors to better blend in with the mudbrick and sandstone that dominated the architecture in Sharakhai's west end. King Zeheb's palace being made of granite, travertine, and marble, she'd decided to wear an outfit of light gray for her mission to spy upon Temel, the King-in-waiting.

She crept along a broad hallway filled with bronze statues and lanterns hung from decorative sconces. She paused to read a plaque mounted on one of the plinths: *Fatima II, Vizira to Our Lord King Zeheb, serving from the 280th year of his reign to the 302nd*. The next was of Baüd, a man who had served as the city's secretary of public works and spearheaded the project to create the city's water reservoir. Others had similar declarations of accomplishments. Mala had never seen Zeheb before, but the statues, renderings of King Zeheb's offspring from his more than four centuries of rule over Sharakhai, gave her a rough impression. They had broad foreheads. Hawk noses. They were *large boned*, as Zeheb apparently was.

Realizing she was wasting time, Mala hurried to the second statue from the end on the right-hand side, and none too soon. She'd no more than stepped behind the statue than she heard voices. They were filtering in from the high, horseshoe archway at the hallway's end. Mala made herself small as two men in rich khalats of green and amber silk passed beneath the archway and into the hall of statues.

"Mark my words," one was saying, "they've returned our Lord King home so he can help with the war effort.

It's why they're in the great hall. They're hoping familiar surroundings will help."

"As you say," said the other, "they surely fear the golems' return, but—"

"Well of *course* they fear the golems' return."

"Yes, but—"

"And mark my words, it's going to happen soon. The Malasani are nearly ready to march again."

"Yes, *but*," the other said loudly as they passed by Mala's hiding place, "*I* heard King Ihsan ordered them away. He used his power on them. So why would they return?"

The first laughed as only the highborn can laugh. "Haven't you heard? King Ihsan was *taken*. He's a captive. More likely the Malasani king has paused the assault while he plies Ihsan for secrets."

Mala breathed a sigh of relief as the heavy doors at the far end of the hall banged shut and their conversation dropped. She immediately began searching the stones behind the statue for the one Shohreh had described to her, the one with the small nick in the corner. When she found it and pressed it, a section of the wall swung inward to reveal a darkened passage. She stepped inside and closed the door, hearing a loud click as the tunnel plunged into darkness.

After days of careful preparation, the Kestrel,

Shohreh, had taken Mala to the mysterious, maze-like set of caverns and tunnels beneath the city. They'd spent an hour traversing those hidden passageways, Shohreh leading them doggedly and confidently ever higher through the caverns and tunnels. All the while it was becoming more and more clear that even walking caused Shohreh pain. And it was growing worse the more she moved.

"It's your rebirth, isn't it?" Mala had whispered, fearful of being overheard in that vast subterranean place.

When Shohreh didn't answer, Mala tugged on her sleeve and repeated the question. Shohreh *was* deaf, Mala had learned, and she was still getting used to making sure Shohreh could see her lips before she asked questions.

Shohreh's answer was a curt nod, but it was the terrible grimace on her face that made it clear just how painful the days after a rebirth were. "It will pass in time."

Eventually they reached a spiraling stairway that led to the lowermost reaches of Zeheb's palace. Shohreh was supposed to take her up, but as she reached the base of the stairs, she set their small lantern down, curled up on the bottom steps, and uttered a long, pitiful moan.

Mala could only stand there, feeling powerless. "Do you need some water?"

"I *have* water," Shohreh managed through gritted teeth, then waved Mala toward the stairs. "Go on without me. You know the way."

Mala shook her head. "We should come back another night when you're better."

"We can't." She curled up and began sucking breath through clenched teeth in the sort of rapid rhythm that spoke of pain spiraling out of control. "Zeheb is being brought there tonight," she said between gasps. "You have to listen, hear what he says. Tomorrow might see King Zeheb being given back to the desert."

Mala felt terrible for leaving her like that, but Shohreh had likely been right. If they were to save King Zeheb from being assassinated by his own family, which would, in turn, save Mala and *her* family, it was crucial they learn more.

In the darkness, Mala's fingers brushed the cold stone walls of the passageway as she shuffled unsteadily toward the palace's great hall. She'd never felt claustrophobic, but she was nervous and the passage was narrow as a goat chute. It made her feel as if the walls were ready to press inward and squeeze the life from her.

Ahead, a pinpoint of light appeared. It grew brighter and brighter the closer she came, until she reached the end of the tunnel and a wide wooden panel, at the center of which was a peephole. Even standing on tiptoes it was difficult to peer through, but she managed it and saw a massive room lit by lanterns hung from tall, pewter stands. This was the palace's great hall, yet not a lick of wood or stone could be seen. Every wall was hidden by thick curtains, the floor a layered sea of carpets. Even the vaulted ceiling was obscured by bolts of cloth—hung as they were beneath the support beams, they looked like the sort of childish waves she used to draw with Jein in the sand.

Luckily, or perhaps it was by design, the peephole itself was situated between two hanging curtains, allowing her a view of the room beyond. In the center of it, a dozen men and women dressed in finery—curled slippers, silk khalats, bejeweled jalabiyas, embroidered abayas and the like—spoke softly with one another. From her vantage behind the wooden panel, Mala could hear only faint reverberations from the women. When the men spoke it sounded louder, like distant thunder.

Not far from the group of highborn stood four Blade Maidens in black battle dresses and turbans. Veils hid their faces. Each had a hand on the pommel of her sword. The King himself sat at the center of the Maidens on a wooden throne. He looked poorly, to say the least. His eyes moved languidly. He was slumped to one side. His lips were moving, though Mala had no idea what he was saying. She doubted the others did, either. They were ignoring him. Whatever they'd brought him here to do, he seemed to be failing at it miserably.

Just then one of the women returned to him while the rest fell silent. With the hall quiet, Mala could just make out her words. "Can you remember, father? Can you remember who were you were listening to?" She was holding up a sheet of papyrus. "'On the night of moonless skies will they kill the Whispering King.' That's what you said. Please tell us who spoke those words."

The woman was surely Anann, Zeheb's daughter and the one most willing to believe that he might one day be cured of his madness. Again and again she pleaded with him, but Zeheb only stared beyond her, through her, his lips moving ceaselessly, caught as he was by the whispers.

"Enough," said one of the men.

This had come from a coxcomb with a pretentious, peacock-feather brooch pinned to the front of his emerald green turban. With his square face, full lips, and a stocky, somewhat ungainly body, he matched Shohreh's description of Temel, Zeheb's son and the would-be King, perfectly.

Anann looked crestfallen. She'd clearly been holding out hope she might find the one responsible for the threat on her father's life. Ignoring her brother, she tried several more times, until Temel placed himself physically between the two of them, forcing Anann to regard him.

"It's time father returned to Eventide. You know how taxing this is for him."

Anann glowered at him. "As if you care about his *comfort*."

She spun and made for the hall's entry doors. Half of the assembled group followed—Anann's allies, Mala supposed. Meanwhile, four servants in Eventide's livery slipped long wooden poles through steel loops in the side of the throne and proceeded to pick Zeheb up and bear him toward the door. The Maidens accompanied them.

Mala dropped down off her tiptoes, relaxing her aching calf muscles. When Shohreh had first mentioned the peephole, Mala had found it strange. The King would certainly have been aware of it, after all. Why would he have allowed it to remain? When Mala asked about it, Shohreh told her it was King Zeheb himself who often went to the peephole to spy on those who'd come to meet with him.

She lifted herself back up and peered at the King sitting so crookedly in his throne. "What a scared little man you must be," she whispered, "to spy on those you call friends."

Just then Zeheb's gaze sharpened. His head lifted and swiveled until he was staring straight at Mala's position behind the wooden panel.

A sheet of cold fell across Mala's skin. She stared into

his eyes for a long while—too long—then finally had the sense to drop down out of sight, just as several of the courtiers were turning their heads to see what had caught the King's attention. *Stupid, Mala. Stupid, stupid, stupid.* The King had heard her. He'd heard her whispers. Now he knew he'd been spied upon.

She was scared to look. She wanted to sprint away and go back home to her mother and Jein and forget any of this had ever happened. But she couldn't. She'd hardly discovered anything yet. And besides, if the King *had* warned the others, it would be better to know how many were coming for her.

She lifted herself back onto her tiptoes and peered carefully through the peephole. King Zeheb was gone, as were the Maidens. The remaining richly dressed men and women were leaving, save two, who stood in silence as the doors boomed shut.

One was Temel. The other matched Shohreh's description of Drogan, an ambitious young man, Zeheb's one-time vizir, now Temel's closest ally. His pointy beard and pronounced chin, coupled with an otherwise-round face, lent a distinct acorn shape to his head.

Temel was staring at the closed doors. "I wish it hadn't come to this."

"Don't feel badly, my lord. You've been more than

patient, but it's time we all face facts. Your father is not only unwell, he's unlikely to ever get better. Pretending otherwise *harms* Sharakhai, not helps it. Ensuring there is someone to rule the affairs of our family unquestioned isn't just prudent, it's essential."

Temel smiled sadly. "Well, we may not have a city to rule soon."

"No," Drogan said with an emphatic shake of his head. "When the Malasani resume their attack, the old walls will hold, and when they do, *you'll* be sitting your father's throne, ready to rule this city as it should be ruled."

"Yes, well…" Temel's voice trailed off. He looked as though he'd rather be doing anything but having that conversation. A moment later, however, he said, "Has all been prepared on that front?"

"It has." Drogan walked to a section of the wall directly across from where Mala lay hidden and pulled aside one of the long curtains, revealing a door with wavy glass panels built into it. He opened it to reveal a lush garden beyond. "After you, my lord."

The two of them left the great hall and entered the garden, their voices fading until Mala could barely hear them. The very thing they were about to discuss was why Mala had come. She'd learned nothing new yet. Not really. She needed to learn not just *who* was going to try to kill Zeheb, but when and hopefully how.

Her fingers trembled as she placed one hand on the cold metal lever that would open the door. She made no move to pull it, however. She courted death by merely having stepped foot in the palace. It felt as if opening the secret door would act like a spell, conjuring up a death sentence.

"Kill her," Temel would say, just as the Crone had, and this time, no miraculous pardon from an infirm Kestrel was going to save her.

Mala's fingers slipped from the lever. She turned. Took careful, soundless steps into the darkness. She'd heard enough, hadn't she? She'd confirmed that Temel and Drogan were conspiring to kill Zeheb. Shohreh could do the rest. *She* was the Kestrel, after all. Who was Mala but a useless gutter wren, a street thief, a girl with a knack for not being seen?

Except there may not be *time*. For all Mala knew they were planning to kill Zeheb that very night. The information she had might not be enough to save him, and if he *was* assassinated, there was no way in the great wide desert that the Crone would listen to Shohreh's promised petition to allow Mala to live. Gods, Shohreh might still kill Mala herself if this all went badly, a thing that would doom not only Mala, but Memma and Jein as well.

So it was that Mala found her footsteps faltering in that cold, dark corridor, then halting altogether. She turned slowly, made her way back to the door, and once more placed the tips of her fingers on the lever. After a deep breath to calm her fraying nerves, she pulled it and snuck into the great hall.

Never had she felt more exposed than she did tiptoeing across the fine, layered carpets. Luckily, the door to the garden had been left cracked open. Mala slipped through it and dropped behind the row of manicured bushes to the left of the door. The twin moons, slim as wood shavings, shone down from above. Several lanterns burned along the palace wall, shedding golden light on Temel and Drogan where they stood speaking near a marble fountain.

And they were no longer alone. There was a third person standing beyond them. A feminine form. It was too dark to make the woman out clearly, but Mala could tell she was wearing a turban.

Bloody gods, Mala thought, *a Blade Maiden.*

It made sense, she supposed. The Kings were all assigned several Blade Maidens as personal bodyguards. Surely Temel, as the King-in-waiting, had received one too. Likely she was as loyal to him as Drogan was. *Mount Tauriyat was like a snake's nest,* the saying went, *fangs and poison everywhere.*

Just then the Maiden bowed to Temel. "Anann has arranged for Zeheb to be broken out of Eventide. Their plan is to do so when the Malasani attack resumes, which looks to be soon."

Temel's reply was lost as he led the three of them toward a low wall, where he motioned to the desert beyond. In the distance, pinpoints of light were arrayed across the dunes, a veil of honey-colored stars. They were the fires of the Malasani encampment, and they were numerous beyond count. Again the voice inside Mala's head screamed for her to leave. She might not know *how* Zeheb would be killed, but she knew when. It would have to be enough.

And yet she found herself drawing more darkness, found herself draping it across her shoulders like a cloak. Moving lithely as a desert fox, she parted the bushes and stepped onto the beautiful green lawn, the lush existence of which warred with everything Mala knew about life in the desert. When she reached the fountain, she could once again make out their voices clearly.

"But look at where they're camped," Temel was saying. "Less than a league from the entrance to the caves. They may already have taken it."

"But they haven't," replied the Maiden. "I've just come from there. The caves remain untouched. The Malasani either don't know about it or have chosen to overlook them for now."

"It still seems odd. Anann must know they'll be spotted and chased, which makes me wonder if your story is true."

"It's all true. I'm certain of it. Why else would your nephew have contracted with a Kundhuni warlord? Why else would the warlord's fleet be waiting to the west, ready to protect Zeheb against any Malasani ships that might follow?"

Temel waved the information away. "Your suggestion is to attack him when he reaches the cavern, then?"

"He'll be most vulnerable on the way there, but since I don't yet know which path they'll take, yes, I think waiting for him in the cavern would be best."

After a moment's consideration, Temel shared a look with Drogan and walked away. He passed within two paces of Mala, thankfully without so much as a glance in her direction. When he was back inside the palace and out of earshot, Drogan said, "Very well. Take Zeheb in the cavern."

He started talking about the particulars—which ship Zeheb would be taken to, where it was situated in the cavern with respect to the others, even the cabin he would likely be given—but Mala was listening with only half an ear. This was it. This was what Shohreh needed. She was saved!

But then, as it often did when she was scared or excited or both, her cloak of darkness slipped. It was only for a long heartbeat, but that was all it took for the Blade Maiden to silence Drogan with a lift of a finger and peer into the darkness. Insects chittered. An amberlark cooed. Time passed in slow, agonizing increments, the worry inside Mala building with each passing moment. Soon it became too much and Mala's cloak slipped again. The Maiden immediately placed her hand on the hilt of her shamshir and began stalking toward the fountain.

Gods, oh gods, oh gods.

Mala didn't know what to do. She wasn't prepared for this. She might sprint for the palace, try to return to the hidden passages, but what good would that do? The Blade Maidens were fleet as falcons. Mala couldn't outrace her.

Think, Mala. Think.

She thought back to the hours and hours of poring over the maps of the palace Shohreh had shared with her, the drilling of possible ways to enter and escape before Shohreh became comfortable that Mala could handle the mission.

The slope beyond the garden wall, Mala recalled, was not a sheer drop—not for some distance beyond the palace, in any case—and yet it was steep enough that she might slide along it quickly and suffer only scrapes.

Reach the wall, Mala. Reach the wall and you stand a chance.

As the Blade Maiden approached, Mala prepared herself.

"Come out, little wren," the Maiden said. "There's no leaving this place now."

As she rounded the fountain on one side, Drogan paced along the opposite, clearly hoping to pinch Mala in place. It was a foolish mistake. Drogan was no warrior. He was a vizir. His reactions would be slow and awkward, a thing Mala could use against him.

While pretending to focus all her attention on the Maiden, Mala shifted toward him. When he reached for her, as she knew he would, she snatched his wrist, lifted his arm high, then pirouetted while twisting hard. In a blink, she was behind him, wrenching his arm up in a tight lock while gripping his khalat with her other hand to guide his movements.

As he cried out in pain, Mala pointed him at the Maiden and shoved him for all she was worth, then sprinted like a springtime hare toward the low garden wall.

She was too scared to look back but could already hear the Maiden's footfalls chasing her, closing the distance fast. It sounded so loud Mala was convinced she was about to be cut down from behind—she could practically *feel* the Maiden's ebon blade slicing through the air—and yet, miracle of miracles, her speed was enough to carry her to the wall.

With a mighty leap off the lip of the wall, she soared through the chill night air. She flew so far that she lost her balance and landed awkwardly. She tried to recover, but it was too dark. She couldn't see the ground properly. She tripped forward and struck the rocky ground hard. She rolled to blunt the impact, as she'd been taught, but it still felt like she was being trampled by a herd of angry oryx.

When her tumble down the steep mountainside finally slowed, she twisted, oriented herself so that her feet faced downslope. Then she was up and running, sliding, teetering down the mountain as she tried desperately to keep her feet.

She'd managed to put a bit of distance between herself and the Maiden, but her pursuer was already closing the distance. The Maiden was twenty paces back, then ten, then five. With the wild glances Mala was sending over her shoulder, she could see the dark length of the curved shamshir gripped in the Maiden's right hand. Against the starswept sky, it looked like a whip held high, ready to lash out.

"Stop now and it will go better for you, girl!"

But Mala couldn't. She was too scared. And in any

case, the Maiden was likely going to kill her. Why make it any easier?

A moment later something struck Mala's right foot, which had the effect of knocking it awkwardly against her opposite foot. She tripped, went flying, arms flailing, and struck the slope face first. Rocks tore into her clothes and skin as she slid and rolled. She managed to right herself, but before she could take another lumbering step downslope, the Blade Maiden caught up and seized her neck in a grip so strong Mala squeaked like a useless, frightened dune vole.

The Maiden forced Mala to face the upward slope and the twinkling lights of the palace. Gods they'd come far in their short flight. "You see how far I've got to drag your sorry hide now?" The Maiden shook her like a mongrel dog with a rat. "I'm tempted to gut you here and leave you for the jackals."

In a fit of wild fury, Mala reached for the knife at her belt. *I'll gut you instead, or at the very least give you a scar to remember me by.* But the Maiden was ready. She snatched Mala's wrist and wrenched it until Mala dropped the knife. As it thumped against the earth, the Maiden backhanded Mala so hard her ears rang and her vision dimmed, obscuring for a moment the moonlit landscape around her.

Suddenly the Maiden's sword lay against Mala's neck.

She could feel the weight of it, could feel its honed edge. She imagined it being drawn across her throat, her lifeblood spilling, the warmth of it draping down along her chest, her belly. A river of it would tickle the skin along her legs. Perhaps that was exactly what the Maiden had in mind. More likely she just wanted to put a scare in her.

Mala would never learn the truth of it, for just then something dark came streaking though the night, embedding itself in the Maiden's shoulder with a meaty thump. An arrow, Mala realized, though where it might have come from she had no idea. The Maiden spun as another clipped her arm, retreated as a third bit into the earth near her feet.

Mala didn't need an invitation to keep running. She turned and fled as more arrows streaked through the night. The Maiden grunted as she retreated further. Soon Mala reached a sheer drop-off and a path that led around a massive shoulder of rock.

"Here," she heard someone whisper. Only a few paces away, Mala spied a form hunkered low. It was Shohreh, moving stiffly, waving Mala closer. "Hurry now."

Mala went, and together they scuttled around the mountain until they were hidden from sight from the ground higher up. The Maiden, thank the gods, gave up

61

the chase. Gods willing, she was dead, but Mala already had a suspicion she wasn't. The fates loved to play their games altogether too much to allow so easy a solution as that.

"You saw a Maiden…" the Crone was saying.

"Yes," replied Shohreh. "She'd gone to the palace to deliver the news."

The two of them were in the map room. Shohreh stood at attention, hands clasped behind her back while the Crone paced before the hearth.

"It's hardly a surprise," the Crone said absently. *"There have long been cracks forming in the sisterhood of the Maidens, Kings choosing daughters unfit to serve."*

The ranks of the Blade Maidens, as the Kestrels, were fed exclusively from the daughters of the Kings. The Crone had never said so, but she seemed to look down on the Maidens, feeling them inferior to the more extensive training of her Kestrels.

It was strange, though. Shohreh had spent nearly her entire life with the Crone. She'd long since learned the subtle clues that shed light on her moods. She looked angry and concerned about Shohreh's news, but less so than the Kestrel would have guessed. Truth be told,

Shohreh had expected her to fly into a rage, but she merely stared into the fire, contemplating.

Shohreh, meanwhile, was doing her best not to seem in as much pain as she actually was. As always after rebirths, the pain was bad, but this time it was coming in waves, and just then she was riding the crest. Her entire body felt like a rag left too long in the sun. Her joints were afire. And her muscles... Gods how they *ached*. They were tight as ratlines, refusing to stretch unless she worked them every waking hour, which only intensified the pain. She wanted go to her bed and curl into a ball until this latest spell passed. She couldn't, though. Let on too much and the Crone would begin to question everything. After all, if she was in so much pain from her rebirth, how had she managed to reach the garden? Was her debilitation what had allowed her to be observed by the Blade Maiden? And how, if her infirmity was so pronounced, had she managed to escape?

The eldest of the Crone's acolytes, Sülten, entered the room. After sending an uncharitable glance in Shohreh's direction, she placed herself so that the Crone's body blocked Shohreh's view of her. Sülten knew very well that Shohreh was deaf and was ensuring her lips couldn't be seen, effectively blocking Shohreh from the conversation.

The two of them spoke for some time. As often

happened when the Crone was deep in thought, shadows seemed to flicker about her head, a strange effect that the Crone had never once spoken about, despite Shohreh having asked her about it many times. "Never you mind, child," she would always say. "Never you mind."

Occasionally Sülten would glance at Shohreh over the Crone's shoulder, an act that made Shohreh extremely uncomfortable. She was certain that whatever Sülten had come about had to do with her mission.

Eventually, having interrogated Sülten to her satisfaction, the Crone sent her away, then rounded on Shohreh. *The girl... You told me you'd killed her.*

"I told you I'd dealt with her. And I have."

"Oh?" More than angry, the Crone looked fiendish, wicked, as if she were about to devolve into the sort of murderous rage she was infamous for. It was the sort of reaction Shohreh had been expecting when she'd delivered the news about King Temel and the Blade Maiden. *"How so?"*

"I'm using her," Shohreh said evenly, which was the only way to approach the Crone when she was in one of those moods. "She has a gift, a gift I decided to use to save your father from the danger he's in."

At the mere mention of her father, King Zeheb, the Crone's eyes relaxed ever so slightly. Her gaze roamed Shohreh's face, trying to ascertain just how much truth lay in her words. *"You were given an order. To kill the girl."*

"An order I've not abandoned. But the truth is we have only days, perhaps mere hours, to stop the son of our rightful King from committing patricide. As much as it pains me to admit, I'm not as fit as I will be in several weeks' time. With at least one Blade Maiden working against us and my sister Kestrels gone, we need all the help we can get. When this is all done, the girl will get her due."

"She'll get her due now," said the Crone.

"High Matron?"

"Your sole focus will be the girl. Her and her band of miscreants. Her and her family."

"But Zeheb—"

"You're unfit for that duty. I'll deal with the Maiden." Before Shohreh could say another word, the Crone turned, her jewelry glinting wildly in the firelight, and strode toward the far tunnel that led to the acolyte's rooms. She paused at the entrance and turned her head so Shohreh could read her lips. *"The girl, Shohreh. You deal with her."*

With that she was gone, leaving Shohreh feeling cold and alone and perfectly heartless.

It was still night when Mala arrived home. Jein was sleeping. Memma was in her rocking chair, snoring loudly, a bottle of cheap araq tipped on its side on the chipped mosaic table next to her. A puddle of liquor glinted on the warped slats of a floor that was otherwise scuffed and dull.

"Oh, gods, Memma," Mala whispered into the chill night air.

The blanket had spilled around Memma's hips, so Mala laid it over her afresh, but the night was chill, so she grabbed another and laid that over her as well. After kissing her mother's cheek, she took the bottle of araq and poured all but a dram's worth through their small window onto the dirty alley outside. Mala had learned not to dump all the liquor. Do that and her mother would blame *her*, but leave a little and she'd think *she'd* drank the rest of it.

Mala knew she probably shouldn't have come home. She should have stayed away for a few days. Shohreh had said that Mala was safe for a time and that she'd deal with the Crone, but Mala wasn't convinced. The Crone seemed like a force of nature, a thing that wouldn't be denied once its course was set. And who was Shohreh anyway but a servant to the Crone's whims?

It was just that Mala had been so lonely. She'd stayed away for a full day after the scare on the mountainside, and she promised herself she'd leave before sunrise. She just wanted, she *needed*, to make sure Jein was all right.

After stripping out of her dusty trousers and shirt and pulling on her night dress, she retrieved one of the cloth-wrapped bundles from the leather purse at her belt. As she lay down in their shared bed, Jein opened her eyes.

"You're back," she said.

"I'm back," Mala replied, and handed her the bundle.

Jein unfurled it and her eyes went wide. "Kanafeh!"

Mala felt terrible about being gone for so long but seeing Jein's smile took away a bit of the sting. "There's another for Memma in the morning. Will you give it to her when she wakes?"

Jein nodded, but she was hardly paying attention. She was already wolfing down the wedge-shaped slice of sweet, sticky, cheesy pastry. It was gone in moments, and she was sucking on her fingers. When she started sucking on the cloth as well, trying to get every last bit of syrup off of it, Mala chuckled at the absurdity of it.

"Will you stop?"

When Jein didn't, Mala snatched the cloth away. Jein only giggled. "It makes my tongue happy!"

Mala giggled with her, which devolved into a long fit of laughter, the sort that built on itself until their stomachs hurt from it. When their laughter had faded, the two sisters huddled close beneath the blankets and Mala said, "Do you promise to give it to her and not eat it? She's hungry, too, you know."

"I know. I promise." Jein snuggled closer. "When are you coming home?"

"Soon," Mala lied. In truth, she had no idea when it would be safe for her to be home.

"Good," Jein said, and they fell asleep in one another's arms.

Mala woke just before sunrise. A warm breeze was blowing. It was going to be a hot day. Leaving Jein curled up, Mala rose and began pulling on her clothes. She'd just belted her trousers when Jein's eyes shot open. She stared about the room as if she had no idea where she was. She seemed frightened. Terrified.

Her head lifted and swiveled until her round eyes landed on Mala. "They're coming," she whispered.

"Who's coming? What are you talking about?"

"I hear them fighting in the hallway. They're coming for me."

"Who?"

"Please," Jein said in an attenuated whisper, "save me."

Mala stood stock still. In that moment, Jein looked like no one so much as King Zeheb when he'd stared at the peephole. She didn't know how the King might have done it, but she was certain King Zeheb was speaking *through* Jein.

Mala felt scared and useless. This was all too big for her. "I don't know *how* to save you."

But Jein's eyes had already begun to lose their crazed look. She whispered no more and curled up in the bed, breathing peacefully, asleep, none the wiser that she'd just been used by one of the Kings of Sharakhai.

Mala threw on the rest of her clothes. She didn't know what to do exactly, but she knew someone who would.

She left her home and sprinted through the streets as the city was waking. She raced along the winding streets of the Shallows, passed through gates into the old city and the merchant's quarter, wended her way through the collegia grounds though it was forbidden to anyone save faculty, students, and their family to enter. Her legs burning, her breath ragged, she finally came to the wide street where the garrison crouched like a bone crusher sleeping off its latest meal.

She stared at it in abject horror. The place was teeming with soldiers: Silver Spears holding pikes, shamshirs, and shields, standing in formation, ten by ten. More men and women wearing plain-looking armor huddled loosely nearby. Even cavalry men on horseback gathered along the collegia's wide lawn. All were listening to a speech being given by a man in bright steel armor on the garrison's front steps.

The Malasani, Mala realized. *They must be preparing for the renewed assault.* No sooner had the thought occurred to her than a great roar came from the south. Gods, the Malasani were already on the march.

Mala needed to find Shohreh. She *needed* to. Her life depended on it. But she was never going to get inside that building. Not today. There were too many people running about.

A man at the head of the cavalry blew a horn, and they set off at a gallop. The Silver Spears followed, then the ragtag infantry.

Maybe after they're gone, Mala thought, then someone grabbed her by her braided hair and yanked her painfully away from the corner of the building she'd been hiding behind. Mala thought a Silver Spear had found her, but it wasn't a Spear. It was Shohreh, dressed in a blood-red battle dress and turban. "Are you trying to get yourself killed?"

"I— I—"

Shohreh shoved her away, toward the Shallows. "Hide, Mala. Hide your family as well. The Crone will be coming for you soon."

"I can't," Mala said, but Shohreh had already turned

away. Feeling like her fate was slipping through her fingers like so much sand, she ran, grabbed Shohreh's arm, and spun her around. "Zeheb spoke to me!"

Shohreh frowned at first, then paused. "You're mad, child."

"It's true! He spoke to me through my sister, Jein."

Shohreh's eyes thinned. "What did he say?"

"He said they're coming for him." She pointed to Mount Tauriyat and the many palaces perched upon its slopes. "He said there was fighting in the halls."

Shohreh stared at the House of Kings. She studied the infantry marching away from the garrison. Then she snatched Mala's wrist and dragged her in the other direction. "Come with me."

Beneath the bright red hull of a racing yacht, Shohreh crouched on the sand, hidden behind one of the two aerodynamic struts that stretched down from the hull to the starboard ski. The skis, made of fabled skimwood, were slick as eel skin, especially against sand, allowing ships to glide easily over the desert.

To her right, beyond a broad towing lane and a curving row of a dozen more sandships, lay the cavern's entrance, which was narrow, barely the width of one of the yachts inside the cavern, but also tall, easily four stories high. The morning's light poured through it, illuminating the cavern, its sandy floor, and the fleet of ships housed within. It was, in effect, a bay of hidden ships.

Beside Shohreh lay a repeating crossbow, already cocked and loaded. Beyond it, crouched behind the same strut as Shohreh, was Mala, her gaze fixed on the mouth of a darkened tunnel, the only other entrance to the cavern. Shohreh's first instinct had been to come alone, but she believed Mala's story—that King Zeheb had somehow spoken to her through her sister. Shohreh didn't know *how* Zeheb had managed it, but she believed he had, and that he might do so again, which was why, despite her better judgment, she'd allowed Mala to come.

Aboard the yacht, two of the crewmen had just finished folding the protective tarp from the deck and stowing it. Three more crewmen were hoisting the sails. Assuming all went as planned, the ship would spirit King Zeheb and his family away, and Shohreh intended to make sure it happened in precisely that manner. As strange as it was to admit, the safest place for Zeheb was far, far away from Sharakhai. Only then would Anann, his daughter, be free to try to heal his addled mind. And whether or not that effort succeeded, she could negotiate for Zeheb's return and ensure his living arrangements wouldn't consist of four stone walls and a locked door beneath Eventide.

As the crew finished setting the mainsail, Mala tugged on Shohreh's sleeve and pointed to the tunnel. A moment later, a large group of people, four of whom bore a litter, came rushing from the shadows. Anann was at their lead. Behind came another of Zeheb's daughters and her barrel-chested son. The litter had its curtains drawn, but surely King Zeheb sat inside it.

On the double they marched over the sand toward the yacht's aft hatch, which had been lowered to the sand. The moment the litter was lost from view, the crew closed the hatch and began pushing the ship on its slick skimwood skis out from its mooring pole toward the towing lane between the ships.

Shohreh could hardly believe her eyes. They were going to escape with hardly a fuss. But how? It all felt too easy. The rogue Blade Maiden knew very well they'd planned to take King Zeheb to the bay of yachts, so where was she? Did she plan to follow the ship, kill Zeheb in the open desert once they were beyond the many eyes of Sharakhai? It was possible, but risky—let the ship go and she might lose them to one of the sandstorms that plagued the open desert.

The ship had just begun to nose out from its sandy berth when silhouettes appeared at the cavern's entrance.

A black arrow came streaking in, embedding itself in the ship's hull near the bowsprit. Storming in through the cavern's entrance were a trio of Blade Maidens on tall horses and a dozen Silver Spears, also on horseback. Behind them, a team of two horses hauled a sleigh on fat skimwood skis with an enclosed compartment at the rear, the sort the city's harbor inspectors used to confiscate contraband or stowaways found on ships.

Archers aboard the yacht readied bows and arrows. Others dropped swords and shields over the side of the ship, which were then taken up by guards on the sand. They proceeded to set up a coarse line of defense against the coming soldiers, but they looked ridiculous, a row of children hoping to stop a charge of mounted knights.

The Blade Maidens, Silver Spears, and the sleigh all came to a stop. Only then did the lead Maiden, a warden, drop her veil and pull her shamshir, a length of curving, ebon steel. She used the sword to point to the ship's hold. *"You have something that belongs to us. Give it back and no harm will come to you."*

"What we have is my father," Anann called from the foredeck, *"and he is no one's prisoner. Now stand aside before this comes to blows."*

Shohreh couldn't hear the tone of her words, but she didn't need to. Annan's body language spoke volumes. She was a proud woman who'd had enough. She was going to take a stand today, for good or ill.

"Your father is a traitor," said the warden.

"That has yet to be proven."

"Only because your father is mad. Come now, Anann Zeheb'ava. Let's be reasonable. No one needs to get hurt over this. In the months Zeheb has resided in Eventide, he has been treated fairly and will continue to be. Give him to us now and I swear to you by sand and by stone we'll find a way to put this behind us."

Anann was neither tall nor regal—she was a *plain*-looking woman under most circumstances—but just then she looked like the Queen of the Desert. *"My father is coming with us. Now make way or my next words will be an order for my men to cut you down."*

The warden's horse was an akhala, a mighty beast with a coat of silver and fetlocks of glinting iron. It threw its head back and shook its mane. It stamped its hooves, thumping the sand as if itching for battle. The warden pulled the reins to bring it back under control. *"That would be a most unfortunate choice."*

Anann stood tall, silent as a gravestone.

The warden looked like she regretted what she was about to do. *"So be it,"* she said, and replaced the veil over her face. At a flick of her hand, one of the Silver Spears behind her spun a clay pot on a rope and launched it high into the air.

As it arced toward the ship, Anann yelled, *"Take cover!"*

Some did. Others released arrows at the Blade Maidens, who had just then kicked their horses into motion. The guards on the sand moved into a rough defensive formation, though what they hoped to do against so many well trained soldiers Shohreh had no idea.

Shohreh reached for the crossbow, but Mala, surprisingly battle ready for her age, was already holding it out for her to take. With a crisp nod, Shohreh took it and raised it to her shoulder. Aiming carefully and gauging the speed of the warden, she pulled the trigger. A thin bolt streaked through the air and pierced the warden's thigh. The horse continued its charge, but the warden herself leaned forward in her saddle, then slumped to one side and fell hard against the sand, victim to the poison Shohreh had laced on the crossbow's small, dart-like bolts.

The flying pot struck the ship's hull. The clay shattered, sending a fine black powder bursting into the air. The cloud it created spread so quickly and was so difficult to see through that the entire ship and those to either side of it were swallowed, lost from view.

Shohreh's aching muscles were slow to respond as she cranked the lever to load another bolt. Pressing the crossbow to her shoulder, she fired again and caught the second Blade Maiden along her back, just above the kidney. Like her leader, the Maiden soon slumped backward, slipped from her saddle, and fell awkwardly to the sand. The third and last bolt narrowly missed the only remaining Maiden, sinking instead into the horse's flank. The horse pulled up and reared, nearly throwing its rider. The Maiden, fighting the reins hard, was soon lost from view, swallowed by the cloud of dust.

The Silver Spears were just heading into the cloud when Shohreh felt a tug on her arm. "What?" she asked Mala, angry over being interrupted.

Mala was jabbing a finger toward the cavern's entrance. *"The sleigh. It's gone."*

Oh gods, she was right. Shohreh scanned the cavern frantically, but the sleigh was nowhere to be seen. Then she caught sight of it, beyond the row of ships across from her, along the far side of the cavern.

It's the rogue Blade Maiden, Shohreh realized. *She means to take Zeheb from under our very noses.* "Stay here," she said to Mala, and began running for all she was worth along the cavern wall, using the moored ships to mask her approach.

As she neared Anann's ship, the cloud of dust was showing its first signs of dissipating—silhouettes of men and women fighting, some near, some distant, could now be seen clearly—but it was still thick enough to hide Shohreh's movements. She skirted the fighting to reach the back of Anann's yacht.

As expected, the hatch was no longer secured, but lowered against the sand. She approached it carefully, ignoring the sweet, amber scent of the dust while peering into the darkness for signs of Zeheb or the rogue Maiden. At the back of the hold, beyond the abandoned litter, a ladder led up to an open hatch and a passageway. Shohreh squinted into the gloom, where several cabin doors were barely visible. At the far end, a body lay unmoving—dead or unconscious, Shohreh didn't know.

She ascended the stairs with care, then advanced with all the caution the situation demanded, yet she was still taken off guard when the hatchway of the nearest cabin door flew open and a figure dressed in the white tabard, mail, and helm of a Silver Spear came flying out.

It was difficult to see in the dimness, but Shohreh could detect a feminine frame beneath the uniform. Surely this was the rogue Blade Maiden in disguise. She bore no sword—the passageway was too narrow to use one effectively anyway. She stepped forward instead and snapped a quick but violent kick into Shohreh's chest. Shohreh tried to block it, but her rebirth and her aching muscles had left her too slow, and she took the full brunt of it.

She flew backwards, arms flailing, into the hold. Her head struck the corner of the enclosed litter. A sharp, blinding pain rocked her skull. A low thrumming filled her deafened ears. As the hold and its open door swam before her, she became vaguely aware of two forms walking past her. The Maiden and… Gods, she couldn't think. Who was the second? Why had she come here?

Slowly, the dizziness faded. The pain ebbed. The dust, having dissipated further, made her painfully aware that precious moments were being lost, but she could hardly stand on her own two feet.

King Zeheb, she finally realized. The rogue Blade Maiden had just snatched King Zeheb.

She stumbled from the hold and looked to her right. Rounding the curve of the long row of ships was the sleigh. It was just entering the final curve toward the cavern's soaring entrance when Mala appeared between two of the ships, sprinting hard toward the sleigh's rear.

Mala, no! Shohreh screamed from within.

The sleigh was moving fast by then. Shohreh thought surely it had pulled too far ahead for Mala to reach it, but at the last moment Mala leapt and grabbed the stairs, which had been swung into their stowed position against the door at back of the enclosed compartment. She'd just pulled herself onto the lip when the sleigh was lost from view.

Pushing the dizziness away, willing her body into motion, Shohreh ran hard between the next two ships. Beyond them, in the cavern's central aisle, was the warden's silver warhorse, waiting dutifully by its charge. Shohreh mounted and kicked the horse into motion. The akhala fought her, but Shohreh was no newcomer to a saddle. She gripped its sides with her legs and held the reins tight, giving the powerful beast no ground, and soon it was obeying her commands and they were hurtling toward the entrance.

They burst from the cavern and into the blinding sunlight, chasing the sleigh at a speed mundane horses could only dream of. The distance closed quickly. Mala, still on the back of the sleigh, held a knife and was using the point against the lock on the door, clearly hoping she might pry it open. Surely realizing it was hopeless, she abandoned the effort, clamped the blade between her teeth, and climbed the back of the sleigh to reach the roof. Once there, she hunkered low, gripping the knife with its point facing down, and stalked forward across the roof.

Breath of the desert, she's going to try to take the Maiden from behind.

Shohreh wanted to scream for her to stop, but doing so would only alert the Maiden, so instead she crouched in her stirrups and whipped the reins across the akhala's rump, urging it into a faster sprint.

Ahead, Mala squatted at the roof's forward edge. The Maiden was on the driver's bench just below her, an easy target, and yet the girl hesitated. She was clearly having trouble summoning her courage.

Good, Shohreh thought. *Leave her to me.*

Shohreh had nearly pulled even with the back of the sleigh when Mala dropped, falling upon the Maiden, stabbing with her knife as she went. How well the knife struck Shohreh couldn't tell, but a moment later, Mala was flying off the driver's bench and onto the sand.

Shohreh was so close by then her horse nearly trampled Mala where she lay, but the beast was trained for war, as any Blade Maiden's horse would be, and leapt over her cowering form. Shohreh finally reached the back of the sleigh and did as Mala had done. She leapt onto the roof, then drew her shamshir.

The Maiden was ready, however. She'd been looking back to see what had become of the girl and saw Shohreh there. She immediately pulled hard on the reins.

Shohreh knew very well she was about to be thrown from the roof, but there were no handholds to speak of and so, as the sleigh swung left, she was swept from the top like slops from a butcher's block. She struck the sand and rolled over one shoulder, tumbling like a wayward boulder. Then she was up and running, sword in hand.

The Maiden was whipping the horses, trying to get the sleigh back up to speed, but Shohreh was coming on fast—too fast for her to escape cleanly—so she abandoned the reins, leapt off the driver's bench, and met Shohreh's fierce first blow with a blinding draw and block of her own ebon blade.

Only then did Shohreh recognize her. "Nadiin?"

By the gods who breathe, it *was* her. The rogue Blade Maiden was no Maiden at all but a Kestrel, one of Shohreh's own sisterhood. But how could that be? The Crone had said they were all gone. Surely that was what Nadiin had *wanted* the Crone to believe—how else to hide her treachery? And yet the very idea of a Kestrel turning traitor seemed ludicrous.

Shohreh thought back to that night on the slopes of Tauriyat. It had been dark. She hadn't been able to see clearly, nor had Mala. Had they been able to, they would likely have seen that the woman speaking with Temel and Drogan had been wearing a *red* battle dress, not black. She would have known from the beginning that a fellow Kestrel was working against her.

Nadiin, grimly silent, pressed her attack, sending Shohreh stumbling backward, forcing Shohreh to use all her energy just to keep her head upon her shoulders.

Nadiin might have won quickly had she been at full strength. But she wasn't. Far from it. A swath of crimson stained her white tabard along one shoulder, evidence that Mala's knife had bitten deep. It was large and wet and spreading quickly. Nadiin was a Kestrel, though. She'd been trained to fight under such circumstances and thundered blow after blow against Shohreh's defenses.

Shohreh might not be wounded as Nadiin was, but the soreness that came with a rebirth in the Sepulchre still weighed on her. It wasn't so bad as it had been in the beginning, though, and it had gotten better with the simple, physical act of running to the ship and riding the akhala hard to catch up to Nadiin.

Nadiin's breath became labored. The copper skin of her face turned pale, surely from the loss of blood. She deftly blocked one of Shohreh's swings, released a battle cry, and unleashed a terrible flurry of blows, but Shohreh had been expecting it. She blocked every wild blow, waiting for her opening. At last, Nadiin took an ill-advised swing at Shohreh's midsection. Shohreh beat the shamshir wide, stepped in, and swung her sword two-handed, up and across Nadiin's guard. It cut deep into Nadiin's side through her ribs.

Eyes wide, Nadiin staggered back, shivering from the terrible blow. She dropped her shamshir and collapsed to the ground, twisting and clutching the wound. She laid both arms over it and pressed, but it would do her no good. A wound like that couldn't be staunched.

Shohreh had hardly noticed the sheer heat rolling across the dunes, but just then, as she stared down into Nadiin's soft, unbelieving eyes, it hit her full force. It felt like the desert itself had taken note of their clash and had felt its heart racing, as Shohreh and Nadiin's hearts had been only moments ago.

"Sister," Shohreh said, old habits dying hard.

"Sister," Nadiin said back.

"Tell me who sent you."

"Who sent *me?"* Nadiin asked.

"Yes." Shohreh waved toward the cavern's entrance in the distance behind her. "Recover a bit of your honor before you die. Tell me who sent you. Tell me who convinced you to turn traitor."

Nadiin split her pained grimace with a smile. *"You always were a bit thick, Shohreh. I'm no traitor."*

"How can you say that? You were ready to kill our Lord King, the man you served since you were a child!"

"I think in time"—she swallowed hard—*"even you'll be able to work it out."*

Just then a gust of wind kicked sand over Nadiin's prone form. In that moment, she went perfectly still. Her eyes went glassy.

Gods, Shohreh thought, *to be so close to solving this riddle only to have Nadiin's death stop her.* She *needed* to know the answer to the question—the *Crone* needed to know—but there was no time to work it through. King Zeheb must be escorted safely from the cavern.

Mala was suddenly there, standing beside her, staring at Nadiin's unmoving form with a look of cold shock.

Shohreh went to the akhala, which had stopped to chew on a bit of ironweed nearby, and took up the reins. "You can't be seen here," she told Mala and held the reins to her. "Take the horse. Skirt the city to the east. Tie it up near the northern harbor, then make your way home."

Mala blinked. She waved at the sleigh. "But the King…"

"*I'll* take care of the King." She helped Mala into the saddle. "Go home. I'll find you when this is all over."

Mala stared at the cavern's entrance behind them, then nodded numbly. She left, cantering toward Sharakhai, a shimmering monument of ochre and kohl, impressive even from this distance. Shohreh, meanwhile, guided the sleigh toward the cavern. One hand raised warily, Anann met her near the yacht. With the Maidens taken down by Shohreh, they'd been able to overwhelm the Silver Spears.

After freeing Zeheb from the locked compartment at the back of the sleigh, they returned him to the ship. He seemed as frail and confused as ever, and spoke only once as he walked up the gangplank. "The Honey-tongued

King! The Honey-tongued King!" he shouted with a crazed expression on his face. "Let's see if it tastes like honey!"

No one knew what he meant by it.

"Thank you," Anann said to Shohreh after she explained what part she'd played in their escape. *"We owe you much."*

Shohreh bowed her head. "I serve at the will of the Kings."

"Yes, well, the Kings are a multi-headed beast. Sometimes their will isn't all that clear, is it?"

Shohreh felt like she'd been struck by lightning. Annan was right. The will of the Kings *wasn't* always clear. They worked at cross-purposes at times, and so did their servants.

Suddenly everything was crystal clear: who had been behind the attacks, who had ordered Nadiin to kill Zeheb. The reasoning behind Shohreh herself being sent to stop it even made a strange sort of sense.

"Are you well?" Anann asked.

"Go," Shohreh said as she ran toward another Maiden's horse, this one a proud copper akhala. "See our King safe."

With that she was on the horse, riding hard for Sharakhai.

As Shohreh had bade her, Mala left the akhala along the quays of the northern harbor, but she didn't go home from there. She had nothing to bring back to her family, nothing to offer besides grief and another mouth to feed. As much as she hated to admit it, she needed to go to Arük. She needed to tell him she'd made things right. She'd make him see, and then she'd ask for a job, any job at all, so she could earn a bit of money. She'd save enough for the medallion from Bakhi's temple. She'd see her mother cured of her ailment.

She went to Arük's grandfather's house, hoping to find Arük there, preferably without Kasha—Arük had never said so, but he liked Kasha, and was always showing off for her, which often meant being cruel to Mala.

When she reached the dusty alley, it was strangely empty. Eerily empty. Normally there were a few dozen locals, children playing, men and women standing about, talking, walking, going on about their lives. But no one lingered, nor stood in the mudbrick archways, nor sat at the sills of their windows, staring down. There was only silence and a slowly building feeling of dread.

Mala came to a shuddering halt when she saw Arük's front door was cracked open. A crude depiction of a red, clawed hand was painted on its beaten wooden surface, the sign of the Crone. Mala had never seen it herself, but she'd heard stories of it, heard about the things that accompanied it. Murderous rages, people screaming, homes choked with the dead.

As she approached, her mouth went dry. The hair on the backs of her arms arose in a sudden, chilling wave. She felt like a walnut was lodged in her throat, and no amount of swallowing could clear it. By the gods who were left behind, the sign was still wet. It had been drawn in blood.

Mala knew she should run, knew she should hide herself somewhere, anywhere, in the city, but she couldn't. She had to know, because if the Crone had done what Mala thought she had, she wouldn't stop there. She would do it to Mala. She would do it to Memma and Jein as well.

She stepped onto the warped wooden porch. She pushed the door open, careful to touch neither the red sign nor the splatters of blood on the door's dry, crumbling surface. Inside the room lay tipped-over tables and furniture left askew.

And blood. Swaths of it. Great, terrible smears of it. In the center of the room, three trails of crimson converged into a river, which led to the back room, the home's simple kitchen.

Lips quivering, hands balled at her sides, Mala approached. And found them. Arük, Kasha, Rennek, and Arük's wizened old grandfather splayed out on the floor in a grotesque display of twisted limbs, torn flesh, and dark innards.

Tears fell from Mala's eyes. Streamed along her cheeks. She heard them patter against the floor, the only sound in the entire city, the entire world.

Until she heard the creak of the floorboards.

Her entire body spasming with fear, she turned to find a figure bathed in shadow at the end of the hall. As Mala watched, the Crone's bent form with her panoply of jewelry resolved from the darkness. "You're not the only one who can wrap yourself in shadow, child."

Mala tried to run. She truly did. But the Crone was already streaking down the hall like a dark revenant. Eyes wide with glee, mouth spread in a toothy leer, the Crone fell upon her.

Shohreh pushed her akhala hard into the city, skirting the growing sounds of battle, wending her way ever closer to the Shallows. She came at last to the street where she'd found Mala, and the place the leader of their pitiful flock called home. It was nearer than Mala's own home and the more likely for her to go to first, so Shohreh had decided to visit it.

The moment she saw the Crone's bloody sign on the door, she knew that whoever lay inside was dead. The leader of Mala's flock of gutter wrens, surely. Likely some of the other wrens as well. Perhaps the grandfather he lived with too.

Her footsteps heavy, Shohreh prayed she'd been wrong, that Mala had gone to her home first, and that it would take time for the Crone to find.

Nevertheless, she stole through the front door. Saw the blood. Saw her hopes dashed. For there, in the sort of twisted display the Crone was infamous for, lay five bodies, Mala's among them. She cried in that small room in the city's poorest quarter. She knelt and lifted Mala to her chest as a bright, burning fury raged inside her. She was furious with herself. Furious with the fates and their cruel ways. Most of all, though, she was furious with the Crone, the woman she'd sworn to protect and obey.

"But one does not owe fealty to the wicked," Shohreh said into the stillness. "Isn't that what the Al'Ambra says?"

She'd given her life to the cause—to protect the Kings and the city above all—and the Crone had twisted it with her perversions, her taste for blood, her thirst for power. No longer. Sharakhai was changing for good or ill. Perhaps it was time for the order of the Kestrels to change as well.

Gazing down into Mala's lifeless eyes, Shohreh wondered if she was ready to go through with this. *Yes,* came a voice inside her. *The time for change has come.*

Hoisting Mala's body over her shoulder, Shohreh carried her to her waiting horse, laid her carefully over the saddle, then mounted and rode west.

A thousand and one visions warred within Mala's mind. Visions of running the streets, of stealing food, of fetching water for a bit of copper, of slitting the purses of strangers and taking out a handful of coins, or cutting a larger hole and sprinting away so that her friends, other gutter wrens, could snatch the coins up when her mark chased after her.

She saw her mother at the first onset of Bakhi's curse. She saw the worry in her eyes, worry over so much more than the pain about to befall her. Memma knew, as did Mala, that their very existence in Sharakhai would be threatened if she wasn't able to bring home the money her work at the carpetmaker's earned.

She saw her sister fetching water from a well, then slipping in because she was trying to reach for the bucket too early. Long terror-filled moments had passed before the local cobbler came running from his shop and helped pull Jein from the well. Her skin was marred by cuts and scrapes suffered during her fall, but she was so happy to be out she laughed nervously, as if it had been her fault she'd fallen in and not Mala's. Mala received a beating that night from Memma, but she didn't care. Jein was safe. That was all that mattered.

A hundred more memories flitted through her mind, but they were slowly replaced by the feeling of weight on her chest, the sensation of immobility. Something was pressing down on her, but what?

She realized she couldn't breathe. She panicked. She fought.

And through her struggles found that whatever was holding her in place was not completely rigid. It gave as she moved. She felt some of the weight being lifted. A hand grasped hers. She was pulled up until the sand— she'd been buried in sand—fell away and she opened her eyes to the sight of the circular room beneath the city, the one with the high ceiling and stone columns and the frieze rendered in a band at the top of the curving walls.

Shohreh was there, kneeling beside the pit, but Mala's mind was so lost in the visions she couldn't say a word. The memories refused to banish themselves, a thousand faces talking to her all at once.

"The madness will pass soon," Shohreh said, helping Mala to her feet.

Mala stared down at her body. She turned her hands over. Stared at her palms. She flexed her fingers, wiggled her toes. "I'm alive."

"You are," Shohreh said with a smile.

"But the Crone. I saw her coming for me... She ... she ... killed me." She took in the room anew, saw the girls standing near the tunnel that would lead them toward the map room. "You brought me back to life."

"I did," Shohreh said, then tugged on Mala's arm until she stepped out of the grave. She ran her hands down Mala's naked body, brushing the sand from her in sheets. Her tangled hair took the longest. Mala wanted to be done with it, but Shohreh was diligent. "This is a precious resource," she said, though Mala didn't really understand what she meant by it.

When they were done at last, Shohreh waved to a rack, where fresh clothes had been laid out. Sirwal trousers. A simple shirt of coarse, tan cloth. Leather sandals. They were not so different from what many children wore in the west end, including Mala, but were made of much finer materials. When Mala was dressed, Shohreh led her from the room, but said to the watching girls in passing, "Clean it carefully, as you always have."

They moved to obey, save one, who stared at

Shohreh, then Mala, beneath softly but deeply furrowed brows.

"You'll do as I've asked, Sülten," Shohreh said, then pinched the girl's ear and tugged hard until she began moving, albeit reluctantly, toward the pit.

Shohreh and Mala retreated to the map room, the one with the complex, topographical map of the city. A fire flickered in the hearth, which Mala went to immediately to chase away the chills. "You saved me," Mala said to Shohreh, making sure to face her as she spoke. "Why?"

"I told you, a life was owed."

"No," Mala said. "There's more to it than that."

Shohreh considered for a time, the firelight playing across her strong chin, her broad cheeks. "Because it wasn't right, what the Crone did to you. But it isn't over yet, child." She pointed to large map of the city, toward the Shallows. "She's still out there. She's looking for your family." Shohreh always seemed like such a powerful woman, but just then she seemed small, unsure of herself. "I'm going to stop her, Mala. Do you wish to help?"

Mala knew exactly what Shohreh meant to do, not the details, of course, but she knew what the result would be. If Shohreh had her way, the Crone would die.

"Yes, I'll help," Mala said resolutely.

"It won't be easy."

"I know."

Shohreh considered her a while, then nodded. "Then come with me."

She turned away, but Mala tugged on her sleeve so she could see Mala's words. "I need something first. A weapon."

"That's not what I need you for, Mala."

"No," she said firmly. "I need this. Take me to Arük's."

Shohreh paused, considering, then nodded. Was there a bit of pride in her look? She led Mala through the tunnels, back to the streets of the western quarter. Once there, they made their way to the Shallows and the sight of the massacre. Mala stepped beyond the door with the red claw upon it and into the sitting room. In the small kitchen, she made her way to Arük, heedless of the blood she was stepping over, and took the jambiya from his belt. It felt heavy in her hands, but also good. Arük had never been very nice to her, but he'd saved her from some pretty bad scrapes too. And he hadn't deserved this. None of them had.

Stuffing the knife into her belt, she turned to Shohreh. "I'm ready."

It had taken time, but eventually the Crone found the home of the girl's mother and sister. She'd given this next step due consideration. Questions might be asked. The young one, Jein, was in fact the daughter of King Mesut, may he find peace in the farther fields. But in the end what matter was that? Mesut was gone and his family would care little for a bastard child from the Shallows.

Dusk had arrived. The snaking alley leading to Mala's home dripped with shadow. Knowing the time was upon her, the Crone put her thumb and forefinger to her lips and whistled in the manner of the Blade Maidens. All scattered.

Alone with her dark thoughts, she drew the shadows in around her and stole toward the door. She reached it and paused, flexing her fingers several times, digging her claws into the palms of her hands while the anticipation built inside her. As she reached out for the handle, a voice called from behind her.

"Stop!"

The Crone turned, knowing who she'd find. Shohreh stood ten paces away, dressed in her red battle dress, her ebon blade held easily in one hand.

"Well, well," the Crone said. "Here you are, fresh from another failure, I presume."

"No failure," Shohreh said as she stepped closer. "I found the King. I saved him from Nadiin. *Mala* saved him."

She let the words linger between them, the implications clear.

"A cancer runs rampant in the House of Kings," Shohreh continued, taking another step over the packed earth, "a cancer that has been growing for centuries, eating its flesh, only now becoming apparent as the Kings' children backstab one another while vying for their fathers' thrones."

The Crone chuckled. "You think you *know* me, girl? You don't. You know less than nothing."

"I know enough. You're a woman who came to see your own father as an impediment. You conspired against him with his son, Temel. You sent Nadiin to kill him. The only thing I couldn't figure out is why you sent *me* to try to save him."

The Crone said nothing. Shohreh could flap that mouth of hers all she wished. The Crone preferred to bide her time, to tug on the shadows and make them ready.

"The only thing that makes sense is that you were undone by Zeheb's whispers. He heard you plotting with Temel, didn't he? He found you out and whispered it aloud, knowing those words would be recorded and read by both you and Anann. He raised the alarm, and when that happened, you couldn't be seen as indifferent. And then *I* showed up, standing on death's doorstep. You saw it as an opportunity. With the other Kestrels supposedly gone from the city, you sent the only resource you had, me. But I was freshly risen from the grave. You *wanted* me to fail. You were counting on it. But if things didn't go as planned, if you and Temel failed to kill your father, you could point to me and say *you'd* been the one to save him."

"Very clever, girl."

"I'm no girl, and your reign ends here."

Shohreh stepped forward warily, lifting her sword as she came. But the Crone was no stranger to battle. And she had more powers than even Shohreh knew about.

She drew the shadows about her, sent them hovering around Shohreh's head and eyes, blinding her. Shohreh immediately retreated, knowing that to remain would make her vulnerable to the Crone's wicked claws.

The Crone followed, wary of the wild swipes from Shohreh's blade. She was patient and needed only the smallest of openings. When it presented itself, as she knew it would, she lunged and clawed Shohreh's armor, ripping leather and skin alike, cutting all the way to bone.

Shohreh grunted against the pain. She rolled away,

retreating farther, rolling back when the Crone struck with another powerful swipe of her claws.

And then she fell. And the Crone swung, a blurring, vicious blow against Shohreh's sword arm. Shohreh's blade went flying.

The Crone cackled. She was about to deliver the killing blow, but paused when she heard footfalls behind her, heard a scream. She tried to pull the shadows in around her but found them strangely resistant. Then they suddenly and inexplicably vanished, and the soft light of the coral sunset returned to that crooked, west-end alley.

The footfalls became a girl with a knife sprinting with abandon toward her. By the gods, it was Mala, the very girl she'd killed only hours ago.

The Crone raised her hand to strike the girl down, but her wrist was caught from behind—Shohreh, the gods damn her. Fearing Shohreh's blade, she dared one glance behind and felt a burning pain in her abdomen. She turned to find the girl twisting a knife, a curving jambiya, deep into her gut.

The Crone hardly moved at all when the girl pulled the knife free. Mala stabbed again, this time between her ribs. She fell to one knee as Mala freed the blood-slicked blade. When she brought the knife down again, it pierced the Crone's neck.

She collapsed to the ground. Blood flowed, hot against her skin. Staring at the brilliant clouds above, she understood. The girl had been reborn. Shohreh had taken her to the Sepulchre. She nearly laughed at the grand irony of it all. All her dreams, undone by a useless little wren, one of her victims returning to kill her in the manner *she* had killed so many others.

She tried to speak, to ask Shohreh what she hoped to do now, but her body failed her.

And then her world went dark.

Shohreh watched as Mala knelt and gave herself over to rage, using the knife to stab the Crone's unmoving form over and over again. Shohreh let it go on for a time—the girl needed to vent some of it lest if fester inside her—but then it became too much. There was a point at which catharsis became something else, something that would one day eat at her soul.

"Enough!" Shohreh said, pulling Mala back. "Enough!"

Mala stood there, breathing heavily, the bloody jambiya gripped tightly in her right hand.

The one saving grace was that Mala, freshly risen from the Sepulchre's grave, wouldn't be thinking clearly just yet. Often the hours and days before and after one's death became hazy over time. Shohreh hoped it would be so for the girl; she didn't deserve to have such memories haunting her forever.

Eventually Mala went still, then turned her eyes on the door to her home, a festive door with childish scribblings rendered in bright purple and yellow paint. *"What now?"* she said.

"That's up to you." Shohreh waved to the door. "You can go on about your life, live it as you please."

"But the other Kestrels might come after me." She stared at the Crone's still form. *"Surely they will after what I've done."*

"I'll do my best to ensure they don't."

"And the other choice?"

"Join me. Join the sisterhood. Become a Kestrel yourself."

Mala stared at her as if she were mad. *"They wouldn't take me. I'm no daughter of a King."* She waved again at the cooling corpse. *"I killed their leader!"*

"Many of the Kestrels are dead. So is the Crone." Shohreh pointed east toward Tauriyat, where a strange glow was emanating. "The rule of this city is about to change drastically, and unless I'm wrong, *we'll* have a say in it. You and I and the others, the acolytes who will one day become Kestrels themselves. We have a chance to forge the path Sharakhai will take."

Mala paused. *"Who will lead us?"*

"I will." She shrugged glancing toward the glow in the east. "Beyond that, I cannot say. Not yet."

"And my family?"

"The families of Kestrels are well cared for. Yours will be as well."

Mala stood there for a long while in the gathering darkness. Then at last, she nodded. *"Where do we begin?"*

Shohreh smiled. "You begin by going to see your family." She reached into her purse and took out a handful of golden rahl. "Get them food. Get them medicine … and *not* the fake medallions they sell in Bakhi's temple. Get your mother to a proper physic. Understand?"

Mala nodded.

"I'll find you, little one." And with that Shohreh turned and began walking away.

A moment later she felt a tug on her arm. She turned to find Mala standing there, looking shy. Then she was rushing forward and wrapping her arms around Shohreh waist, enveloping her in a fierce hug. Shohreh had become a stranger to touch. She'd forgotten how good it felt. Slowly, as the walls of her discomfort began to crack, she gave in to the feeling and squeezed Mala back.

"Thank you," Mala said when she broke away. Then

turned and went into her home.

Long after the door had closed, Shohreh stood there, wishing she could hear their reunion.

Then she smiled and lost herself in the streets of Sharakhai.

Twelve Kings in Sharakhai is the first book in The Song of the Shattered Sands series, an epic fantasy with a desert setting, filled with rich worldbuilding and pulse-pounding action.

Sharakhai, the great city of the desert, center of commerce and culture, has been ruled from time immemorial by twelve kings—cruel, ruthless, powerful, and immortal. With their army of Silver Spears, their elite company of Blade Maidens and their holy defenders, the terrifying asirim, the Kings uphold their positions as undisputed, invincible lords of the desert. There is no hope of freedom for any under their rule.

Or so it seems, until Çeda, a brave young woman from the west end slums, defies the Kings' laws by going outside on the holy night of Beht Zha'ir. What she learns that night sets her on a path that winds through both the terrible truths of the Kings' mysterious history and the hidden riddles of her own heritage. Together, these secrets could finally break the iron grip of the Kings' power...if the nigh-omnipotent Kings don't find her first.

A sample comprised of the book's first chapter follows...

Chapter 1

In a small room beneath the largest of Sharakhai's fighting pits, Çeda sat on a wooden bench, tightening her fingerless gloves. The room was cool, even chill compared to the ever-present heat of the city. Painted ceramic tiles lined the walls. A mismatched jumble of wooden benches and shelves that had clearly seen decades of abuse made it feel well loved if not well cared for. Were Çeda any other dirt dog, she would have sat in one of the rooms on the far side of the pits, the ones that hosted dozens of men and women. But Çeda was given special dispensation, and had been since winning her first bout at the age of fourteen.

By the gods, five years already.

She tightened her hands into fists, enjoying the creak of the leather, the feel of the chain mail wrapped around the backs of her hands and knuckles. She checked the straps of her armor. Her greaves, her bracers, her heavy battle skirt. And finally her breastplate. All of them had once been dyed white—the color of a wolf's bared teeth—but now the armor was so well used that much of the leather's natural brown shone through. *Well and good,* Çeda thought. It felt used. Lived in. Kissed by battle. Exactly the way she liked it.

She picked up her bright steel helm and set it on her lap. She stared into the iron mask fixed across the front—a mask of a woman's face, cold and expressionless in the face of battle. Affixed to the top of the helm was a wolf's pelt, teeth bared, muzzle resting along the crown.

Echoing down the corridor came a voice that sounded old and hoary, a mountain come to life. "They're ready." It was Pelam.

Çeda glanced toward the arched doorway with the blood-red curtains strung across it. "Coming," she said, then returned her attention to the helm. She ran her fingers over the many nicks in the metal, over the mask's empty eyes—

Tulathan grant me foresight.

—stroked the rough fur of the wolf's pelt—

Thaash guide my sword.

—then pulled the helm over her braided black hair and strapped it tightly on.

As the weight of the armor settled over her, she parted the heavy curtains and hiked up the sloping tunnel into the heat of the noontime sun. The walls of the fighting pit towered around her, and above them, arranged in concentric circles, were the seats of the stadium. *It's going to be a good day for Osman.* Already there were several hundred waiting for the bout to begin.

Roughly half the spectators called the city of Sharakhai home; they knew the pits inside and out, knew the regular dirt dogs as well. The other half were visitors to the desert's amber jewel. They'd come to trade or find fortune in a city that offered greater opportunities than they'd had back home. It rankled that so many came here, to Çeda's home, and lived off it like fleas on a dog. Though she could hardly complain—

A boy in a teal kaftan pointed to Çeda wildly and called, "The White Wolf! The Wolf has come to fight!" and the crowd rose to their feet as one, craning their necks to see.

—the pits paid well enough.

A ragged cheer went up as she strode to the center of the pit and joined the circle of eleven other fighters.

The money men in the stands began calling out odds for the White Wolf. She hadn't even been chosen to fight yet, so no one would know who her opponent would be, but many still flocked to be the first to wager their coin on her.

The other dirt dogs watched Çeda warily. Some knew her, but just like those in the audience, many of these fighters had come from distant kingdoms to try their hand against the best fighters in Sharakhai. Three women stood among those gathered—two well muscled, the third an absolute brute; she outweighed Çeda by three stone at least. The rest were men, some brawny, others lithe. One, however, was a tower of a man wearing a beaten leather breastplate and a conical helm with chain mail that lapped against his broad shoulders. Haluk. He stood a full head and a half taller than Çeda and stared at her like an ox readying a charge.

In response, Çeda strode toward him and pressed her thumb to an exposed edge on the back of her mailed gloves. She pressed hard enough to pierce skin, to draw blood. Haluk stared at her with confusion, then a wicked sort of glee, as Çeda stopped in front of him and pressed her bloody thumb to the center of his leather breastplate.

The crowd roared.

A new flurry of betting rose, while the rest of the

audience jockeyed for position against the rim of the pit.

Çeda had just marked Haluk for her own, an ancient gesture that not all dirt dogs would respect, but these would, she reckoned. None of them would wish to fight Haluk, not in their first bout of the day. When Çeda turned away and returned to her place in the circle, all but ignoring Haluk, the naked anger on his face was slowly replaced with a look of cool assessment. *Good,* Çeda thought. He'd taken the bait and would surely choose her if she didn't choose him first.

When some but not all of the betting flurry had died down, Pelam stepped out from another darkened tunnel. The calls of betting rose to a tumult as the audience saw the first bout was ready to begin.

Pelam wore a jeweled vest, a brown kufi, and a red kaftan that was not only fashionable but fine, save for its hem, which was hopelessly dusty from its days sweeping the pit floors. In one of Pelam's skeletal hands he held a woven basket. As the fighters parted for him, he stepped to the rough center of their circle and flipped the basket lid open. After one last check around him to ensure all was ready, he shot his hand into basket's confines and lifted a horned viper as long as his lanky legs. The snake wriggled, swelling its hood and hissing, baring its fangs for all to see.

Pelam knew his business, but the snake made Çeda's hackles rise. Bites were rare but not unheard of, especially if one of the fighters was inexperienced and jumped when the snake drew near. Çeda knew enough to remain still, but foreigners didn't always follow Pelam's careful pre-bout instructions, and it wasn't always the person who jumped that the snakes chose to sink their fangs into.

As Pelam held the writhing snake, each of the fighters spread their legs wide until their sandaled or booted feet butted up against each other's. After a glance at each of the fighter's stances, and finding them proper, Pelam dropped the snake and stepped away.

It lay there, coiling itself tightly. The crowd shouted to the baked desert air, their voices rising to a fever pitch as each yelled the name of their chosen fighter. The fighters themselves remained silent. Oddly, the snake slithered toward Pelam for a moment, then seemed to think better of it and turned to glide over the sand to Çeda's left, then turned once more. And slithered straight through Haluk's legs.

Silence followed as a pit boy ran and snatched the viper by its tail, lowering it back into its basket as the snake spun like a woodworker's auger.

Pelam calmly awaited Haluk's choice.

The big man didn't hesitate. He made straight for

Çeda and spat on the ground at her feet.

The crowd went wild. "The Oak of the Guard has chosen the White Wolf!"

Oak indeed. Haluk was a captain of the Silver Spears, and a tree of a man, but he was also a particularly *cruel* man, and it was time he learned a lesson.

Like jackals to a kill, the news drew spectators from neighboring pits. The stands were soon brimming with them.

As the rest of the fighters exited the pit, a dozen boys jogged out from the tunnels bearing wooden swords and shields and clubs. Çeda, as the challenged, would normally be allowed to choose weapons first, but she followed ancient custom; she had marked him, and thus *she* was the true challenger, not Haluk, so she bowed her head and waved to the weapons, granting first choice to Haluk. Most would have returned the honor, but Haluk merely grunted and chose one of the few weapons meant for both him and his opponent: the fetters.

The noise of the crowd rose until it was akin to thunder. Some laughed, others clapped. Some few even stared with naked worry at Çeda, who had clearly just been put at a severe disadvantage by Haluk's choice of weapon.

The fetters was a length of tough, braided leather. It

was wrapped tightly around one of each fighter's wrists, keeping them in close proximity and ensuring a brawl.

While glaring intently at Haluk, Çeda held out her left hand, allowing Pelam to slip the end of the fetters around her wrist and tighten it. Pelam did the same to Haluk, then took a small brass gong and mallet from one of the boys.

The pit was cleared so that only Çeda, Haluk, and Pelam remained.

The doors to the tunnels closed.

And then, after a dramatic pause in which Pelam held the gong chest-high between the two fighters, he struck it and stepped away.

There was slack in the fetters, a situation Haluk would quickly attempt to remedy—his best hope, after all, lay in controlling Çeda's movement—but Çeda was ready for it. The moment Haluk lunged in to grab as much of the leather rope as he could, she darted forward, leaping and snapping a kick at his chin. When he retreated, Çeda charged, a move he clearly hadn't been expecting. His eyes widened as Çeda grabbed his clumsily raised arm and sent her fist crashing into his cheek.

She could feel the chain mail dig deep into the fighting gloves she wore, but it was worse for Haluk. He fell unceremoniously onto his rump, his conical helm flying off and thumping onto the dry dirt, kicking up dust as it went.

The crowd stood and howled its delight.

As his helm skidded well out of reach, Haluk rolled backward over his shoulder and came to a stand, so quickly that Çeda had no time to rush forward and end it.

Haluk raised one hand to his cheek, felt the blood from the patterned cuts the mail had left in his skin, then stared at his own hand with a look like he'd disappointed himself. And then his eyes went hard. He'd been pure bluster before, trying to intimidate Çeda, but now he was seething mad.

None so blind as a wrathful man, Çeda thought.

Haluk crouched warily and began wrapping the fetters around his left wrist, over and over, slowly taking up the slack. Çeda retreated and pulled hard on the fetters, putting her entire body into it, making the leather scrape painfully along Haluk's arm. He ignored it and continued to wrap the restraints around his wrist. Çeda yanked on the fetters again, but he blunted the tactic with well-timed grips on the leather, the muscles along his arm rippling and bulging. He grinned, showing two rows of ragged teeth.

Çeda sent several kicks toward his thighs and knees, attacks meant more to test Haluk's reflexes than anything else. Haluk blocked them easily. She was just about to yank on the fetters again when he loosened his grip and rushed her. Çeda stumbled, pretending to lose her balance, and when Haluk came close she dove to her right and swept a leg across his ankles.

He fell in a heap, the breath whooshing from his lungs.

He grabbed for Çeda and managed to snag her ankle, but one swift kick from Çeda's free heel and she was up and dancing away while Haluk rose slowly to his feet.

The crowd howled again, many of the foreigners joining in, though they had no idea why. The Sharakhani knew, though. They understood why bouts like this were so very rare.

Haluk hadn't been defeated in more than ten years of fighting in the pits. Çeda had rarely lost since her first bout, and she'd lost none in the past three years. Everyone knew how widely the story of this bout would be told, especially if Çeda took him in so cleanly a fashion. Few would dare utter the tale within Haluk's hearing, but the entire city would be alive with it by the end of the day.

And Haluk knew it. He stared into Çeda's eyes with an intensity that reeked of desperation. He would not be so easy to take again.

As the two of them squared off once more, the crowd went completely and eerily silent. The only sound was of Haluk's ragged breathing and Çeda's strong but controlled breaths from within the confines of her helm.

Haluk took one tentative step forward. Çeda stepped away, snatching up some of the slack in the fetters as she went. Haluk did the same until they both held a quarter of the length in reserve, leaving them a scant few strides from one another.

Haluk took two measured steps toward her. He was trying to close the distance, but he was no longer reckless. He was cautious, as a man who'd become a captain of Sharakhai's guard *should* be.

Çeda kicked at his legs again, connecting but doing little damage. That wasn't the point, though. She had to keep him on his guard until she was ready to move in. She snapped another kick and retreated, but she could only go so far. Haluk had drawn up more of the fetters, so Çeda released some of hers. Haluk strode forward, taking up more of the braided rope. Which forced Çeda to release more. Until she had none left.

He drew sharply on it, keeping his center low, his balance steady, and Çeda was drawn forward until she was just out of his striking range.

The crowd began to stamp their feet, the sound of it reverberating in the pit, but otherwise they were silent, rapt.

Haluk pulled again, harder now that they were so close. And that's when Çeda moved.

Using the tension on the fetters to pull herself forward, she launched herself with a leap, straight into his body. In his surprise, Haluk grasped for her neck, but she slipped her forearms inside his and grabbed two fistfuls of his lanky brown hair. She wrapped her legs around his waist, twisted them around his thighs, and locked her feet around his knees, hoping to trip him up and end this once and for all.

He didn't fall, however. He was too big. Too strong. And he did exactly what she would have done. He rose up, preparing to slam her against the ground.

At the high point of his lift, she did the only thing she could: she clung hard to his neck and waist.

When they came down, they came down hard. Pain burst across Çeda's back and rump as Haluk's full weight bore down on her. Through her coughing and the ringing in her ears, she could hear him laughing. "Foolish move, girl."

He tried to lift away, but she'd locked her arms around his neck. Her legs hugged tightly to his waist. He was strong, but he had no leverage to break her grip. Again and again he tried to lift himself away from her to give himself room to punch, but each time he did, she began slipping her arms around his neck to cut off his blood. He would drop to prevent it, and then they were back, body to body, breath coming hard and fast, the very intimate duel continuing as each struggled for any small amount of leverage.

Once, when he lifted his head too far away, she crashed her forehead against his. The lip of her helm left a long cut against his skin. Blood seeped down his forehead, along his nose. It pattered against her steel mask, filling her nostrils with the smell of it.

Then, in a sudden and furious move, Haluk lifted, slipping a forearm across her throat, managing to pin her down.

Immediately the crowd was up, shouting, raging. But it all became little more than a keen ringing in Çeda's ears. She heard her own heart thrumming. Felt Haluk's arm tighten further.

It was a strong move, a *wise* move under the conditions, but he'd left himself open. She slipped her right hand down along his left arm, near his elbow, where she'd have the most leverage, and pushed. She let out a guttural cry while muscling his arm up, which had the effect of propelling herself down along his body, just enough to slip her head under his armpit and out of the lock.

He tried to slip his arm back under her neck, but before he could, she grabbed the buckles along the far edge of his breastplate and hauled herself away, and now she was halfway to his back. Exactly where she wanted to be.

She reached her left arm—the one tied to the fetters—up and over his head. The rope slipped neatly down along his face and across his neck. Immediately she tightened her grip and drew the fetters back.

Haluk knew what was happening—he tried to throw her off, at least enough to get his fingers beneath the fetters—but her grip was too sure. Still, he was a bull of a man. She grunted while gritting her teeth and arching her back. Her arms strained like cording on a ship's sails.

She thought surely he would have pounded his hand against the ground by now, giving up the match, or fallen unconscious, but he hadn't. He still struggled for air, his breath coming out in a desperate hiss, his mouth frothing from it. And then finally, all at once, his body went slack.

Çeda didn't hear the strike of Pelam's gong, marking the end of the bout.

But the crowd she heard.

Their elation could no longer be contained. They stomped their feet. They shook their fists. "The Wolf has won! The Wolf has won!"

Ignoring them, Çeda pushed Haluk onto his back

and straddled his chest. She unwrapped the fetters and saw the blood drain from him, casting his face in a strange, deathly pallor.

His eyes blinked open. He stared into Çeda's eyes with a look of confusion, then took in his surroundings as if he had no idea where he was. The roaring crowd and Çeda's masked face soon registered, though, and a look of deep and inexpressible anger stole over him.

Çeda leaned down until they were chest-to-chest and whispered into his ear. "The next time you take your hands to your daughter, Haluk Emet'ava"—she pressed the thumbnail of her right hand into his side, in the depression between his fourth and fifth ribs— "it will go much worse for you." She leaned closer still and whispered, "The next time, it will be a knife in the dark, not a beating in the light." She rose, her legs still straddling him, and stared down into his eyes. "Do you understand?"

Haluk blinked. He made no acknowledgment of her demand, but there was shame in his eyes, a shame that spoke the truth of his crimes better than words ever could.

Like a wedge driving ever further into a thick piece of wood, she pressed her thumb deeper. "I would hear your answer."

He grimaced against the discomfort, licked his lips,

and glanced to the cheering crowd. Then he nodded to her. "I understand."

Çeda nodded back, then stood and stepped away.

Pelam had watched this exchange with a glint in his eye that landed somewhere between curious and concerned, but he made no mention of it. He merely turned and presented Çeda to the crowd with a bow of his head and a flourish of his hand. As some howled and others collected their winnings, Çeda was surprised to see that Osman himself had come to watch—Osman, the owner of these pits, a retired pit fighter himself, the man she'd had to trick to earn her first bout.

How far we've come since then.

He stood with the crowd on the topmost row. He was one of the very few—along with Pelam—who knew her true identity. She had no idea how long he'd been watching, but surely he'd caught the end. She couldn't tell if he was pleased or not. Çeda gave an exaggerated nod to the crowd, but she and Osman both knew it was meant for him.

He nodded back, then tugged his ear, which meant he wished to speak.

To speak, and perhaps more.

With Blood Upon the Sand is the second book in The Song of the Shattered Sands series, an epic fantasy with a desert setting, filled with rich worldbuilding and pulse-pounding action.

Çeda, now a Blade Maiden in service to the kings of Sharakhai, knows the dark history of the asirim, that hundreds of years ago they were enslaved to the kings against their will. When she bonds with them as a Maiden, she feels their pain as if her own. They hunger for release, they demand it, but with the power of the gods compelling them, they find the yokes around their necks unbreakable.

Çeda hopes to free them, but the need for secrecy has never been greater. After the victory won by the Moonless Host in the Wandering King's palace, the kings are hungry for blood. They scour the city, ruthless in their quest for revenge. Unrest spreads like a plague, a thing Emre and his new allies in the Moonless Host hope to exploit, but with the kings and their god-given powers, there is little hope of doing so.

When Çeda and Emre are drawn into a plot of the blood mage, Hamzakiir, they sail across the desert and learn a devastating secret, one that may very well shatter the power of the hated kings. They plan to take advantage of it, but it may all be undone if Çeda cannot learn to navigate the shifting tides of power in Sharakhai and control the growing anger of the asirim that threatens to overwhelm her.

A Veil of Spears is the third book in The Song of the Shattered Sands series, an epic fantasy with a desert setting, filled with rich worldbuilding and pulse-pounding action.

Since the Night of Endless Swords, a bloody battle the Kings of Sharakhai narrowly won, the kings have been hounding the rebels known as the Moonless Host. Many have been forced to flee the city, including Çeda, who discovers that the King of Sloth is raising his army to challenge the other kings' rule.

When Çeda finds the remaining members of the Moonless Host, she sees a tenuous existence. Çeda hatches a plan to return to Sharakhai and free the asirim, the kings' powerful, immortal slaves. The kings, however, have sent their greatest tactician, the King of Swords, to bring Çeda to justice for her crimes.

But the once-unified front of the kings is crumbling. The surviving kings vie quietly against one another, maneuvering for control over Sharakhai. Çeda hopes to use that to her advantage, but whom to trust? Any of them might betray her.

As Çeda works to lift the shackles from the asirim and save the thirteenth tribe, the kings of Sharakhai, the scheming queen of Qaimir, the ruthless blood mage, Hamzakiir, and King of Swords all prepare for a grand clash that may decide the fate of all.

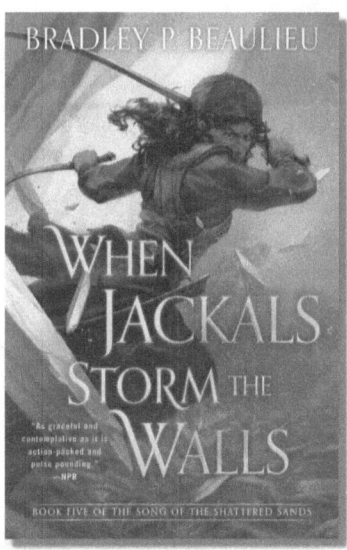

When Jackals Storm the Walls is the fourth book in The Song of the Shattered Sands series, an epic fantasy with a desert setting, filled with rich worldbuilding and pulse-pounding action.

The reign of the kings of Sharakhai has been broken. The blood mage, Queen Meryam, now rules the city along with the descendants of the fabled twelve kings.

In the desert, Çeda has succeeded in breaking the asirim's curse. Those twisted creatures are now free, but their freedom comes at great cost. Nalamae lies dead, slain in battle with her sister goddess. Çeda, knowing Nalamae would have been reborn on her death, sets out on a quest to find her.

The trail leads Çeda to Sharakhai where, unbeknownst to her, others are searching for Nalamae as well. Çeda's quest to find her forces her into a terrible decision: work with the kings or risk Sharakhai's destruction.

Whatever her decision, it won't be easy. Sharakhai is once more threatened by the forces of the neighboring kingdoms. As the powers of the desert vie for control of the city, Çeda, her allies, and the fallen kings must navigate the shifting fates before the city they love falls to the schemes of the desert gods.

Of Sand and Malice Made is the exciting prequel to *Twelve Kings in Sharakhai*, the acclaimed first novel in The Song of the Shattered Sands.

Çeda is the youngest pit fighter in the history of Sharakhai. She's made her name in the arena as the fearsome White Wolf. None but her closest friends and allies know her true identity. But this all changes when she crosses the path of Rümayesh, an ehrekh, a sadistic creature forged aeons ago by the god of chaos.

Çeda flees the ehrekh's attentions, but that only makes Rümayesh covet her even more. Rümayesh grows violent. She threatens to unmask Çeda as the White Wolf, but the danger grows infinitely worse when she turns her attention to Çeda's friends. Çeda is horrified. She's seen firsthand the suffering left in Rümayesh's wake.

As Çeda fights to protect the people dearest to her, Rümayesh comes closer to attaining her prize and the struggle becomes a battle for Çeda's very soul.

This spellbinding tale is sure to strike a chord with readers of Peter V. Brett, Brent Weeks, and Trudi Canavan—as well as fans of Twelve Kings in Sharakhai eagerly awaiting the later books in the Shattered Sands series.

This omnibus edition of The Lays of Anuskaya is comprised of *The Winds of Khalakovo*, *The Straits of Galahesh*, and The *Flames of Shadam Khoreh*, and two Lays of Anuskaya novellas: "To the Towers of Tulandan" and "Prima."

Among inhospitable and unforgiving seas stands Khalakovo, a mountainous archipelago of seven islands, its prominent eyrie stretching a thousand feet into the sky. Serviced by windships bearing goods and dignitaries, Khalakovo's eyrie stands at the crossroads of world trade. But all is not well in Khalakovo. Conflict has erupted between the ruling Landed, the indigenous Aramahn, and the fanatical Maharraht, and a wasting disease has grown rampant over the past decade. Now, Khalakovo is to play host to the Nine Dukes, a meeting which will weigh heavily upon Khalakovo's future.

When an elemental spirit attacks an incoming windship, murdering the Grand Duke and his retinue, Prince Nikandr, heir to the scepter of Khalakovo, is tasked with finding the child prodigy believed to be behind the summoning. However, Nikandr discovers that the boy is an autistic savant who may hold the key to lifting the blight that has been sweeping the islands. Can the Dukes, thirsty for revenge, be held at bay? Can Khalakovo be saved? The elusive answer drifts upon the Winds of Khalakovo…

Find more adventures in other worlds with *Lest Our Passage Be Forgotten & Other Stories…*

With *The Winds of Khalakovo*, Bradley P. Beaulieu established himself as a talented new voice in epic fantasy. Now, with the release of his premiere short story collection, Beaulieu demonstrates his ability to weave tales that explore other worlds in ways that are at once bold, imaginative, and touching. *Lest Our Passage Be Forgotten & Other Stories* contains 17 stories that range from the epic to the heroic, some in print for the first time.

Twelve Kings in Sharakhai marked the start of a bold new epic fantasy series for critically acclaimed author Bradley P. Beaulieu.

In the Stars I'll Find You & Other Tales of Futures Fantastic features Beaulieu's science fictional work, from exploring far-flung worlds to finding what it means to be human through artificial intelligence to the cost of dividing ourselves—or ourself—through the use of technology.

In this short story collection, you'll find eleven tales that explore our very human relationship with technology, some in print for the first time.

The Burning Light is a stand-alone novella by Bradley P. Beaulieu and Rob Ziegler.

Disgraced government operative Colonel Chu is exiled to the flooded relic of New York City. Something called the Light has hit the streets like an epidemic, leavings its users strung out and disconnected from the mind-network humanity relies on. Chu has lost everything she cares about to the Light. She'll end the threat or die trying.

A former corporate pilot who controlled a thousand ships with her mind, Zola looks like just another Light-junkie living hand to mouth on the edge of society. She's special though. As much as she needs the Light, the Light needs her too. But, Chu is getting close and Zola can't hide forever.

A thrilling and all-too believable science fiction novella from the authors of Twelve Kings in Sharakhai and Seed.

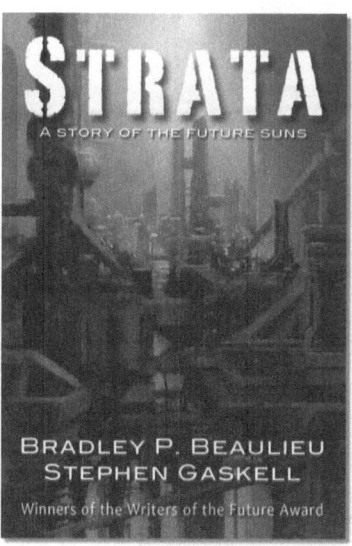

Strata is a stand-alone novella by two Writers of the Future Award winners.

It's the middle of the twenty-second century. Earth's oil and gas reserves have been spent, but humankind's thirst for energy remains unquenched. Vast solar mining platforms circle the upper atmosphere of the sun, drawing power lines up from the stellar interior and tight-beaming the energy back to Earth. For most, life is hard, cramped—and hot.

Kawe Ndechi is luckier than most. He's a gifted rider—a skimmer pilot who races the surface of the sun's convection zone— and he needs only two more wins before he lands a ticket home. The only trouble is, Kawe's spent most of his life on the platforms. He's seen the misery, and he's not sure he's the only one who deserves a chance at returning home.

That makes Smith Pouslon nervous. Smith once raced the tunnels of fire himself, but now he's a handler, and his rider, Kawe, is proving anything but easy to handle. Kawe's slipping deeper and deeper into the Movement, but Smith knows that's a fool's game. His own foray into the Movement cost him his racing career—and nearly his life—and he doesn't want Kawe to throw everything away for a revolt that will never succeed.

One sun. Two men. The fate of a million souls.

ABOUT THE AUTHOR

Bradley P. Beaulieu fell in love with fantasy from the moment he started reading *The Hobbit* in third grade. From that point on, though he tried reading many other things, fantasy became his touchstone. He always came back to it, and when he started to dabble in writing, fantasy—epic fantasy especially—was the type of story he most dearly wished to share.

Twelve Kings in Sharakhai, the first book in his latest series, The Song of the Shattered Sands, was named to over twenty "Best of the Year" lists when it was released in 2015. His critically acclaimed series, The Lays of Anuskaya, has recently been released in omnibus form.

Brad, who recently became a full-time writer, lives in Racine, Wisconsin with his wife and two children. Beyond writing, cooking has become an obsession. His favorite dishes are French, Italian, and Mexican/Southwestern, but he is also fascinated by the art of bread baking.

For more, please visit www.quillings.com